THIS BOOK IS DEDICATED TO ANYONE
WHO'S EVER BEEN TOLD OFF FOR
DRAWING IN THEIR SCHOOL BOOKS.

I FEEL YOUR PAIN.

Acknowledgements

Thanks to my girls for being a constant supply of funny stories
and sticky situations – I have either been inspired by them
or outright stolen them to use in this book.

Thanks to the real-life Geraldine and Gerald Puffins for
all your hard work, in particular, Kelly, Katy and Wendy.

Thanks to Antony Topping for helping to make Trixie a thing.

Thanks to all the children, teachers, librarians and dinner ladies
from the schools that I have visited with my books – you have
inspired me, encouraged me and fed me in equal measures.

And a special thanks to all the viewers of my Art Club during
the different lockdowns – it was a strange time but
together we made it a bit more fun.

CHAPTER 1

TROMBONER SQUEEZER

Hello, readers! I want to start this book by telling you that art sucks. There you go, I've said it — ART IS SUCKY.

Although when I say 'There you go, I've said it — ART IS SUCKY' it's not really me saying that; it's the person who I was before all the stuff that happens in this book happened (which I guess is technically still me, but it's not the me who is currently talking to you right this minute).

Sorry for such a complicated beginning — it's just my way of letting you know that I USED to be like a lot of you: I USED to think art was boring.

SO LET ME GET THIS STRAIGHT. I'M THE OLD ME WHO THOUGHT ART SUCKED . . .

. . . AND I'M THE ME FROM NOW WHO THINKS ART IS COOL.

AND I'M A TALKING CARROT, IN CASE THIS BIT WASN'T CONFUSING ENOUGH.

Don't get me wrong — I really like drawing. If you ask me, some of my cartoons should qualify as art, but my art teacher, Mr Woodhouse, doesn't agree. He discovered my 'Teachers of Wormwood High Reimagined as Insects' drawing in the back of my book and he gave me after-school detention cleaning paintbrushes. I dread to think what he'd be like if he saw any of my actual comic strips (I'll show you some of those later on in this book).

You can't really blame me for being down on art — Mr Woodhouse's classes are dull. Have you noticed how some teachers know that their subject is boring, so they go over the top to try to make it fun? Unfortunately for me, Mr Woodhouse is the exact opposite.

I reckon he must have made a bet in the staffroom about how many kids he can get to fall asleep in his class (his record is four, by the way). Every lesson, he brings in random objects from home and we have to sit in a circle and draw them. I swear sometimes he forgets to bring in stuff and we actually draw whatever he can find in his car.

WHAT ARE YOU WAITING FOR?

GET DRAWING!

NO-FREEZ

D.RINK

FRESH

When we aren't drawing his random rubbish, he teaches us about what he calls 'proper art'. I think he has the word 'proper' confused with 'mind-numbingly dull'.

His lessons are always about fusty old paintings of miserable kings and queens and other posh people I've never heard of. To borrow my best friend Beeks's catchphrase, his 'proper art' can 'get in the bin'.

Mr Woodhouse used to go on about how amazing Leonardo da Vinci's *Mona Lisa* is — apparently everyone always says her smile is 'enigmatic'.

Actually, before we go any further, I need to point out that this book contains some words that you might not know the meaning of — like 'enigmatic'. I've done this on purpose because my mum only lets me read books if they 'develop my reading' and 'expand my vocabulary'.

THIS ISN'T JUST ANOTHER TRASHY FART BOOK, IS IT, JOHNNY?

WHAT A PERTINENT QUESTION, MOTHER. THIS BOOK IS IN FACT EXORBITANTLY EDUCATIONAL.

If your parents thought that this was just a really funny book with loads of jokes and farts in it, they probably wouldn't buy it for you.

Hi, this is Geraldine Puffin, owner of Puffin Books, here. I just wanted to tell you not to worry as this IS still a really funny book with loads of jokes and farts in it.

GERALDINE PUFFIN

Hi, Gerald Puffin here, Geraldine's husband, chipping in to let you know that this book also contains two of the funniest toilet-related stories you're ever likely to hear. That's all from me for now. Speak again soon! Enjoy the book – bye!

GERALD PUFFIN

As well as sprinkling a few unusual words throughout this book, I've also made some fact files about the different artists that I mention, but I promise it's only the not-boring stuff.

FACT FILE:
LEONARDO DA VINCI

He painted the *Mona Lisa*.

He used to cut up dead bodies and draw them.

HELLO AGAIN!

Looks like a wizard

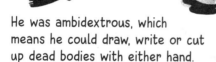

He was ambidextrous, which means he could draw, write or cut up dead bodies with either hand.

He was obsessed with the proportions of the human body.

He drew this famous diagram called *Vitruvian Man*, which I think looks like a human octopus.

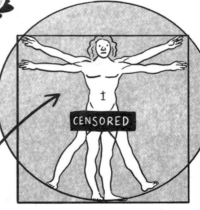

CENSORED

IF ANY ADULTS ASK, THIS BOOK IS ACTUALLY QUITE EDUCATIONAL.

HA HA! HE LOOKS RIDICULOUS!

Anyway, where was I? Oh yeah, Mona Lisa's smile being enigmatic. 'Enigmatic' is just another word for mysterious, and people have never been able to work out whether Mona Lisa is actually smiling or not, AND, if she is smiling, no one knows exactly what she's smiling about.

I have my own theory. I think Mona Lisa had just let out a really squeaky fart and that smile of hers is actually a mixture of relief, because the fart had been trapped indoors for so long, and embarrassment, because it made such a weird noise. A noise like a trombone being played badly.

BETTER OUT THAN IN!

SQUEEEEEJJJJ!!!

It's for this reason that, instead of calling her Mona Lisa, I call her Tromboner Squeezer. Beeks did a tromboner in maths class once that went on for so long that Mr Davidson, the supply teacher, thought it was a fire alarm and made us all queue up in the playground.

On the whole, though, despite what the me from the first sentence of this book said, the me from now doesn't think art sucks any more. In fact, it does the opposite, whatever that is. Art blows?

No, rewind. I'm pretty sure if you say something blows that's also bad. Here you go: I think art neither inhales or exhales. Glad we cleared that up.

Right, in the next few chapters I'm going to tell you all about why I no longer think art is boring and I'll also fill you in on the secret double life that I now lead.

Buckle up and get comfy, or, if you prefer to
be uncomfortable, go and sit on a hedgehog,
because we're about to begin.

OH, GREAT.

LEAVE ME
OUT OF THIS.

CHAPTER 2

A BIT ABOUT ME, A BIT ABOUT BEEKS AND A BIT ABOUT GEEGEE

Apart from the fact that I recently turned twelve, my life is pretty ordinary. In fact, I'M pretty ordinary. I'm like the 99.99 per cent of children who don't have a book written about them. My main goal each day is to navigate my way through school without showing up on the bullydar (that's the radar all bullies seem to have that helps them spot which kids to pick on).

I'M AFRAID, ACCORDING TO MY BULLYDAR, YOU NEED TO GIVE ME YOUR LUNCH MONEY.

BEEP BEEP

SIGH.

My other main goal is not to call my teacher 'Mum' by mistake again. You don't live that sort of thing down quickly. Luckily for me, when I did it, it happened the same day that Dudley Davis had his 'greatest' moment.

When Dudley got dressed after PE, he managed to get both of his legs through one underpant hole. He walked kind of crab-like for the rest of the day, which was OK until he got called up to the front of the class to read. He shuffled out of his chair and after only two steps he fell and banged his head on the corner of a table.

He was out cold for about ten seconds and when he came round his first words were: 'Can we ride on the teacups again, Grandma?' After that, me calling the teacher 'Mum' was quickly forgotten.

Like I said, I'm pretty average. I'm not the fastest runner (that would be Beeks) or the one all the boys want to go out with (that's Gretchen Heron).

I'm not the one all the girls want to go out with (Spencer Smedley) or the one all the teachers want to adopt as their own child (Ernest Wozniak).

I'm not the school maths genius (Suranna Adebayo) or the opposite of genius (Dudley Davis), and I'm not the one who reached the size of a fully grown adult and started shaving by the age of ten (Rory McGory) or the one who rips up your homework and threatens to give you a turbo noogie if you tell on him (also Rory McGory).

I CALCULATE THAT DUDLEY HAS A 73.6 PER CENT CHANCE OF GETTING BULLIED.

WHAT'S A 'PER CENT'?

HEY, CRUDLEY! HOW QUICKLY CAN YOU RUN INTO MY FIST?

SURANNA ADEBAYO

DUDLEY DAVIS

RORY McGORY

I suppose if I did have to be a 'the one', I'd be the one who can draw funny cartoons. Although, as I mentioned earlier, that particular skill does get me into trouble. Last year my parents got called into school because Mrs Harris found a comic strip I'd drawn in the back of my workbook that she called 'highly offensive'.

It was all about how aliens were slowly taking over the school by kidnapping the teachers and replacing them with exact replicas.

BEHOLD, MY BEAUTIFUL ARMY OF CLONE TEACHERS.

PERFECT IN EVERY DETAIL.

Everyone found it easy to tell which teachers were the clone teachers though, because the aliens missed a small but crucial detail. They had given their clones minty-fresh breath, which, as we all know, real teachers don't have.

I FIND THIS HIGHLY OFFENSIVE.

WELL, YOU ARE DEFINITELY NOT A CLONE!

This isn't one of those books where the main character has a special power. My only superpower is being completely average.
Well, that and being able to burp the alphabet (although it's always hit-and-miss whether or not I bring up a little bit of sick around the 'ellamennopee' bit).

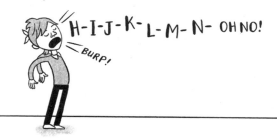

H-I-J-K-L-M-N- OH NO!

BURP!

This also isn't one of those books where the hero's parents are dead, missing, cursed by zombie witches, abducted by aliens or really into chess. They only do that sort of thing in books to make you sympathize with the main character.

BRAAAIINS!

HELLO AGAIN!

DO EITHER OF YOU TWO FANCY A GAME?

ZOMBIE WITCH   ALIEN   CHESS NUT

There's no need to sympathize with me, as my parents are very much alive and well. I live at home with both of them, plus there's also my older brother, Travis, and my little brother, Dylan.

Travis used to go to Wormwood High too, but he left a few years ago. A lot of the teachers who taught him now teach me, which, believe me, is not a good thing.

Dylan is only in preschool and even though he's incredibly annoying I do kind of feel sorry for him. By the time HE gets to Wormwood, the teachers are gonna REALLY have it in for him.

LET'S CUT TO THE CHASE AND GET YOU BOOKED IN FOR SOME DETENTIONS. HOW DOES EVERY TUESDAY AND THURSDAY SOUND?

Someone else you need to know about is Beeks. He lives two doors down and he's my best friend, although sometimes you wouldn't know it. It all depends whereabouts on the Friendship Frisbee™ you catch us. (I was going to call it the Friendship Cycle, but that sounds like something out of a school textbook, plus alliteration ALWAYS makes stuff better.)

We are currently in the Good Place, thanks to some pretty crazy stuff we got up to together over half-term.

Me and Beeks have been friends for as long as I can remember. Our mums have loads of pictures of us growing up together, including this one particular photo that they always use as a bargaining tool.

Superman has kryptonite, vampires have garlic and crosses (or both at the same time if you stick two garlic baguettes together) and Beeks and I have the 'playing in the garden sprinkler naked' photo.

Mum even wrote a really cringey caption on her copy. Let's just say, if it were to ever see the light of day, it would definitely not be a good thing.

Beeks and Trixie's First Date!

Whenever Mum wants to make me do something, she threatens to send that picture into the *Wormwood Post*'s 'Photo Funnies' page.

Her threats are powerless now though, because I found out where she kept the family photo album and I peeled out that awful picture. It's now safely hidden away in my Top-Secret Documents folder and THAT is safely hidden away in my Top-Secret Hiding Place. I have to find places in my room to hide my stuff because my little brother, Dylan, is always snooping around. If I ever shout at him though, he turns on the waterworks and Mum and Dad instantly take his side. They protect him like he's some kind of endangered animal.

MUMMUM, TRIXIE SHOUTED AT ME.

TRIXIE!

Dylan has found most of my hiding spots but, if you pull out my bottom drawer completely, there is a gap underneath that he doesn't know about. It's where I keep all my super-important stuff.

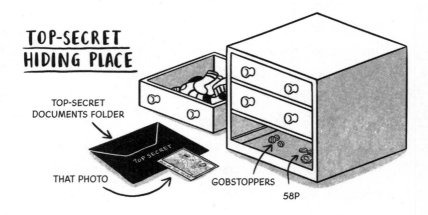

TOP-SECRET HIDING PLACE

TOP-SECRET DOCUMENTS FOLDER

THAT PHOTO

GOBSTOPPERS

58P

Anyway, back to Beeks. Even though he's a boy, he's a pretty good best friend. BUT he is also SUPER gullible. I once told him that when you learn something new, if you want your brain to remember it, you have to keep it trapped inside your head.

The week we learned how to multiply fractions, Beeks spent the best part of three days walking around school with his fingers in his ears.

He recently had a growth spurt, making him the second tallest in our year, but he's also super awkward and uncoordinated, like a baby giraffe wearing roller skates.

The only other person I need to tell you about for now is Auntie GeeGee. She is my mum's sister and, because she doesn't have kids of her own, she spoils us whenever she gets the chance.

I guess it's a bit like when you look after the school rabbit. You only get it one weekend a year so, when you do have it, you treat it like rabbit royalty. I'm guessing that if you had to sweep chocolate raisins out of its hutch 24/7, then you'd probably treat it the same way Mum treats us.

Her real name isn't GeeGee, by the way – I just couldn't say 'Georgina' when I was little and it kind of stuck. Lucky her name wasn't Penelope, I suppose.

AUNTIE PEE PEE!

Anyway, this story sort of starts on my twelfth birthday. Everyone came round after school to give me presents in exchange for a slice of cake. Grandma and Grandad got me a hoodie that I'd seen in Hadderley's and had told Mum I really liked. They got it three sizes too big though, so I could 'grow into it'. This was an incredibly Grandma-and-Grandad thing to do.

WE GOT IT IN AN XXL.

THANKS.

HAPPY BIRTHDAY

When the doorbell went and I saw it was
Auntie GeeGee, I started to get really excited.
GeeGee always comes up with the goods in the
present department.

Last year she got me the latest *Axe Maniacs*
game and a voice-changing megaphone, so I had
high hopes for this year. I started to imagine
what she might've got me.

AXE MANIACS VI?

FIRST-EDITION
MUTANT MOUSE?

ROBOCOPTER?

When she said that she was taking me to an art exhibition, I thought she was playing a joke on me. As I waited for GeeGee to pull out the real present, I looked round to see if Mum and Dad were videoing this hilarious prank.

They weren't, and there was no real present. This was it. No *Robocopter*, no *Axe Maniacs VI*, no first-edition *Mutant Mouse* comic. I was going on a lame trip to a fusty museum with my auntie to look at portraits of Henry the Whatever and his however-many wives. It was at that point I started to suspect it was ME who had been cursed by zombie witches, and

AUNTIE GEEGEE was the one who had been cloned by aliens.

Luckily I've had a lot of practice perfecting my 'I'm genuinely happy' face, so I don't think GeeGee sensed my disappointment.

This awesome treat was three LONG school days away — how would I cope with the wait? (That was sarcasm, by the way.)

CHAPTER 3

DINOSAUR CARNAGE

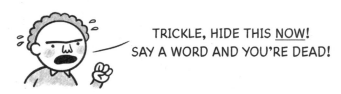

TRICKLE, HIDE THIS <u>NOW</u>!
SAY A WORD AND YOU'RE DEAD!

These were the words of an out-of-breath Rory McGory as he stampeded round the corner into the lower playground and hurriedly shoved something into my bag.

KEEP IT ZIPPED, TRICKLE!

It was Friday lunch break and I'd almost gone a full week without attracting the attention of Wormwood High's top bully.

Most kids scarper when they see Rory McGory coming — like those small grass-eating dinosaurs when they spotted a T-Rex.

COME BACK AND GIVE ME YOUR LUNCH MONEY!

ERM, PLACES TO GO, PEOPLE TO SEE.

'Trickle' is Rory's nickname for me. It doesn't sound too bad till you realize it's actually short for 'Pixie Trickle', which he says is the noise a fairy makes when it's having a wee.

PIXIE TRICKLE

CAN'T A FAIRY HAVE A WEE IN PEACE?

TRICKLE!

Rory has names for everyone. Suranna Adebayo is 'the Adebayo-bot 3000', Ernest Wozniak is 'Ernie Buttsuck' and Spencer Smedley is 'Captain Perfect'. Poor Dudley Davis has it worst though: he is 'Chudley Davis', 'Crudley Davis' and 'Spudley Davis'. Sometimes Rory likes to get creative.

MUDLEY DAVIS!

Beeks is the only one Rory doesn't have a nickname for. Beeks says it's because Rory is scared of him, but I think it's more likely that Rory couldn't think of a name that sounds more stupid than 'Beeks' already does.

IT'S NO GOOD. THERE'S NOTHING THAT SOUNDS MORE STUPID THAN 'BEEKS'.

('Beeks' is short for 'B.K.' – his full name is Bryan Kobi O'Neal. I think, if Rory DID want to call him something embarrassing, 'Bryan' would be much worse.)

Anyway, back to the playground. Closely following Rory round the corner was Mrs Chowdhury, wanting to know where 'it' was. I guessed 'it' was whatever Rory had just shoved in my bag. Rory acted all innocent while Mrs Chowdhury searched him, and she found nothing. She sighed and walked away with all the enthusiasm of a jaded cop who's retiring in a month and just wants a quiet life.

Rory McGory slapped me on the back just a bit too hard and said . . .

When he was gone, I looked in my bag and found David Andrews' comfort dinosaur ripped into several pieces. It was dinosaur carnage!

David Andrews was in his first week at
Wormwood and he had no friends because
his family had only just moved to the area.
His mum and the teachers had let him keep
a stuffed toy dinosaur with him so he didn't
feel sad.

As I gave David Andrews back the torn pieces,
I felt kind of sorry for him, but I couldn't help
thinking the grown-ups were partly to blame.
He would have been less of a target if he'd had
an actual target with the words 'BULLY ME' on
his back.

However much David Andrews' mum and the teachers weren't helping matters though, the real problem was Rory. He made going to school a nightmare — if only there was something I could do about him . . .

WELCOME TO . . . BULLY ISLAND!

BULLY ISLAND

My brain busily dreamed up ways to stop the T-Rex from terrorizing the grass-eaters till it was rudely interrupted by the end-of-lunch bell. Only a few more hours of school and it would be time for my amazing art-exhibition birthday present with Auntie GeeGee — I couldn't wait.

ALSO SARCASM.

CHAPTER 4

ART EXHIBITION? MORE LIKE FART EXHIBITION

School had finished, I was on a train with GeeGee and I wasn't exactly doing cartwheels about this whole art-exhibition thing. Which was lucky because if I was actually doing cartwheels on a moving train I'm pretty sure I'd be sick. I can't even read in the car without feeling like my stomach is doing a washing-machine impression. Thinking about it, if I did cartwheels on a train AND burped the alphabet I would 100 per cent vom.

H-I-J-K-L-M-N-EURRGH!!!

Anyway, I'm getting sidetracked with all this cartwheel/train/sick talk. My point is, I wasn't looking forward to the boring art exhibition. GeeGee started to tell me that it wasn't going to be like a normal art gallery and that I might actually like it. In my head I had been picturing lots of dead-posh people looking at paintings of dead, dead-posh people, with everyone making 'mwah' noises as waiters handed out weird tiny snacks from silver trays.

SAUTÉED KANGAROO BUMHOLE, MADAM?

MWAH! DON'T MIND IF I DO.

GeeGee said the exhibition wasn't even being held at an art gallery — we were going to a disused warehouse and all the artists were 'street artists'.

She pulled a book out of her bag and said it was also part of my present. It was filled with all the artists that we were about to see.

She flicked to one artist who looked quite cool. He makes pictures using lots of tiny coloured tiles, and his art is nearly always based on video-game characters, like Mario or Pac-Man. He glues his mosaics to the sides of buildings late at night and doesn't always ask for permission from the building owners first. To stop himself getting into trouble, he keeps his true identity hidden and goes by the made-up name 'Invader'.

That is a pretty common theme among the street artists in the book: they nearly all have weird-sounding made-up names.

FACT FILE: INVADER

He's a French
street artist.

He makes mosaics
of video-game
characters from
tiny tiles.

IT'S-A ME!

He doesn't really
look like this —
that's a mask.

He sticks his artwork
on to buildings at night.

His name comes from
the old arcade game
Space Invaders.

No one knows who he is
or what he looks like.

He also makes
pictures using
Rubik's cubes.
(He calls it
Rubikcubism.)

GLUE

When we got to the warehouse, it was massive! It was also the complete opposite of everything I'd expected. There were no weird snacks on silver trays, no one was shushing you to be quiet, and the art was actually fun. Some of it was more than fun — it was funny!

There was work by a French guy called Blek le Rat, who does lots of stencils — mainly of rats doing stuff like taking selfies and singing into microphones.

He also made this really funny picture of a chimpanzee proudly standing with his arm round a framed picture of a banana. It made me think of my older brother, Travis!

One wall was completely covered in blue handprints. It looked like a random mess from up close, but when you stepped back you could see the handprints made a picture of an elephant on a skateboard.

COOL!

I KNOW, RIGHT?

There were loads of Invader mosaics dotted around the place, including a huge Sonic the Hedgehog, some droids from *Star Wars* and loads of aliens from *Space Invaders*.

The artist I liked most, though, was called Banksy. He makes loads of really funny spray-painted pictures. There was one of some gangsters firing guns, but he'd swapped their guns for bananas. There was another one that showed a guard from Buckingham Palace going for a sneaky wee up the side of a wall. There was even a version of the *Mona Lisa*, except he'd swapped her 'enigmatic' face for a big smiling emoji.

He didn't just use spray paint either. Right in the middle of the warehouse was a replica of Stonehenge that he'd made out of portable toilets.

AWESOME!

It reminded me of the time I balanced six fun-sized Snickers on top of each other and called it *The Leaning Tower of Peanut*. I was already an artist and I didn't even know it!

TA DAA!

If Mr Woodhouse had been around to see all this, he would've had kittens!

THIS IS <u>NOT</u> PROPER <u>ART</u>!

CONGRATULATIONS, MR WOODHOUSE. IT'S A BEAUTIFUL, HEALTHY LITTER OF KITTENS.

The thing I like most about Banksy is that he uses his art to stick up for people who don't have a voice. Also, he isn't afraid to ridicule the people in power. If politicians or megacorporations do bad stuff, Banksy will create art that makes them look stupid.

It's like he's an art superhero, and that gave me an idea. Maybe, just maybe, I could solve the Rory McGory problem using the power of ART.

CHAPTER 5
THE PLANNING FOR THE PLAN

Some people have fancy ideas but never follow them through. Dad used to say that one day he was going to camp out in the front garden and wait for whoever was letting their dog poo outside our house, then follow them home and post the poo through their letter box. But he never did it.

SPECIAL DELIVERY!

He also used to say 'How would they like it if I pooped right outside their front door?' Thankfully he never did that either.

ISN'T THAT DEREK PICKLE FROM NUMBER 17?

YES, AND HE APPEARS TO BE UNDOING HIS TROUSERS.

One thing you can say for me, though, is that when I get an idea in my head I fully go for it. Like the time I decided the floor was lava and I didn't touch the ground for four days.

TRIXIE!

THIS IS SERIOUS, MUM . . .

THE FLOOR IS LAVA!!!

Inspired by my new hero, Banksy, my plan was to sneak into school at night and create an artwork that would show up Rory McGory as the bully he is.

However, I must admit that there were moments over the next few days when I had second thoughts about it all. Yes, Rory was a bully who EVERYONE at school was scared of, but was I going too far? Was Rory REALLY that bad? Those second thoughts were soon silenced during geography on Tuesday morning.

Mr Atwal was in the middle of teaching us about different kinds of rivers when Rory threw a screwed-up piece of paper at Beeks's head.

Beeks opened it up and, just as he started to read what was on it, Mr Atwal shouted in his direction.

SIR, I THINK BEEKS IS WRITING NASTY THINGS ABOUT ME.

Mr Atwal grabbed the paper and read it out loud.

MR ATWAL HAS BOGEYS IN HIS BEARD. PASS IT ON!

Beeks tried to protest his innocence, but Mr Atwal wasn't having any of it – Beeks lost his morning break for the rest of the week and he had to go and stand outside the deputy head Mrs McGovern's office.

That was it – the final straw. My blood was boiling and any doubts I'd had about whether or not my Banksy plan was too extreme were gone.

Rory was a marked man. (Well, technically he was a marked boy but you wouldn't know it from looking at him — he can watch 18-rated movies at the cinema without getting questioned.)

ONE TICKET FOR *ULTRA-VIOLENT CHAINSAW KILLERS III* PLEASE, YOUNG MAN.

TICKETS

ULTRA-VIOLENT CHAINSAW KILLERS III

CERTAINLY, SIR.

Before I could carry out my plan, I needed to do a bit of planning for the plan. Obviously I didn't want to get caught, so I decided to take a leaf out of Banksy's book. Banksy is like a ninja: one day there's a blank wall, the next morning there's a cool artwork, and no one ever knows how it got there. I needed an outfit that would help me stay in the shadows, so I settled on my black jeans and black jumper. I also made a mask out of a black T-shirt that I'd got from a bag of clothes going to the charity shop.

It was Travis's favourite band
T-shirt till Mum
accidentally shrank it
down to a quarter of
its original size. Travis
complained at the time,
but Mum pulled out the
'If you're not happy, you can
always do your own laundry' line.

I didn't feel TOO bad about cutting up a T-shirt
that was supposed to be going to the charity
shop though. Mainly because it was only big
enough for a toddler now, and there can't be
many two-year-olds really into the music of
King Radish and the Savage Rabbits.

HERE, YOU CAN
HAVE THIS NOW.

ERR, NO THANKS.
I PREFER JAZZ.

RANDOM
TODDLER

The following Monday, at lunchtime, I snuck into the art department at school to look for some chalk spray. (Unlike spray paint, chalk spray easily brushes off. I wanted to be a rebel but I didn't want to be a rebel who ended up in prison.)

I thought the coast would be clear because Mr Woodhouse had been off school for a couple of weeks. There was a rumour going around that grumpy old Woodhouse had died after slipping on a vegetarian sausage and now his ghost was haunting the canteen. But I think that was just something Rory had made up.

The art classroom wasn't empty though. Instead, a youngish lady wearing dungarees and a knotted headscarf was standing at the sink, scrubbing paint off her hands.

OH, HI!

HELLO!

She introduced herself as Miss Handley, the substitute art teacher. Apparently Mr Woodhouse wasn't dead – his wife got five numbers on the lottery and they were on a six-month alpaca-tracking holiday in Peru.

LOOK, GEOFFREY – ALPACAS!

AMAZING.

Miss Handley asked why I wanted chalk paint so I told her all about Banksy and the exhibition and said I wanted to make my own street art at home (obviously I left out the part about my plan to ridicule Rory). She was actually OK about it. She gave me the cans of chalk spray and she also gave me another art book to read at home.

She'd put sticky notes next to the artists she thought I might like - including this one called Bridget Riley.

FACT FILE:
BRIDGET RILEY

She is famous for painting swirly black-and-white patterns.

Her style of art is called (op art.)

Because her paintings are like optical illusions.

Rock bands from the 1960s wore T-shirts with her art on them.

MY HEAD HURTS!

Staring at her art for too long can make you feel dizzy.

(Some people have even been sick!)

You know how sometimes you get those teachers who are a million miles away from being cool but still try to act cool to get kids to like them? Well, I think Miss Handley might actually be the real deal. She even said I could come back any time if I needed art supplies.

TRY-HARD TEACHER

YO, KIDS – I'VE MADE A RAP TO HELP YOU LEARN THE ORDER OF THE PLANETS.

MISS HANDLEY

SURE, HELP YOURSELF TO WHATEVER YOU NEED. ALWAYS HAPPY TO HELP OUT A BUDDING ARTIST.

I needed one more thing before I could get on with my plan: a cool name. I wanted to sign my artwork, but obviously I couldn't use 'Trixie Pickle'. I needed something catchy, so everyone would remember the name of the artist behind this mission to ridicule Rory.

I'm sure the more intelligent among you have already worked out what I decided to call myself. For the rest of you, here are a couple of clues.

Firstly, I like alliteration and, secondly, the name's on the cover of this book in big letters. That's right: I called myself the Art Avenger.

OK, readers, that's enough about how I planned the plan. It's time for me to tell you how I executed the plan.

LET'S DO THIS!

BLACK MASK (USED TO BE TRAVIS'S FAVOURITE T-SHIRT)

BLACK JUMPER

DARK RUCKSACK (ACTUALLY GREEN BUT YOU CAN'T TELL AS THIS IS ALL BLACK AND WHITE)

CHALK SPRAY

MORE CHALK SPRAY

BLACK JEANS

SKETCHBOOK

CHAPTER 6

THE ART AVENGER

It was a few days later and Mum and Dad were out, so Grandma and Grandad were babysitting. This meant sneaking out would be a piece of cake. (I don't like calling it 'babysitting' because Travis and me definitely aren't babies any more. I still think the term applies to Dylan, but if you ever call him a baby he starts to cry. If anything, this just proves my point!)

I AM <u>NOT</u> A BABY!!

Travis was upstairs in his room listening to his music. He's got a 'KEEP OUT' sign on his door but, to be honest, the smell coming out of there does the job much better than any sign ever could.

STINKY FUG!

KEEP OUT!

Dylan was downstairs doing horse riding on Grandma's knee while Grandad watched TV. There was a local news report on, about a statue of one of the Wormwood brothers that was being pulled down from outside the town hall.

THE STATUE OF THE DISGRACED JEREMIAH WORMWOOD IS SET TO BE PULLED DOWN LATER THIS MONTH.

FASTER, GRAMGRAM!

I told them I'd be upstairs in my room studying. I could tell they were only half listening but that suited me fine.

I got into my Art Avenger outfit and crept out of the house. I only had to go round the corner to get to school but, to make sure I went undetected, I did my best ninja walking (a bit like normal walking but far stealthier).

After a few minutes, I reached the bit of loose
fence just along from the General's kennel.
The General is the world's most miserable dog.
He belongs to Mr James, the school caretaker,
and he's sort of an unofficial therapy dog.

I guess the thinking is that once you see how
sad the General is, you feel slightly better
about your own problems.

WOW, I REALLY
COULD HAVE IT
MUCH WORSE.

Mr James lives in a bungalow on the school grounds, and the General is supposed to stay in his little side garden bit, but occasionally he ventures out.

THE GENERAL'S KENNEL

MR JAMES'S BUNGALOW

Travis told me that one time, when HE was at Wormwood, the General escaped and stole one of Mr Bootle's flip-flops. There was a hilarious chase, with the huge hairy PE teacher hopping and swearing across the playground. Travis said Mr Bootle looked like a caveman trying to catch a wild boar.

COME BACK!

UGG!

Nowadays, though, the General mostly just trudges around his shabby kennel looking sad. The liveliest thing he ever does is to sit on the grass outside the science block and lick his private parts while you try to learn about solids, liquids and gases.

I kind of felt sorry for him when I saw him slumped in front of his kennel, but it made my job of sneaking into school undetected a lot easier.

I headed to the lower playground, got the chalk spray out of my rucksack and started painting. I had to climb on top of one of the big bins to reach the higher bits. I guess the lid wasn't on properly, though, because it slipped out from under my feet and I fell in.

OH, FISH STICKS!!!

Luckily it was filled with bin bags, so it was a comfy landing. Unluckily, when I tried to climb out, my foot went all the way to the bottom and got soaked in bin juice. I finished the rest of the picture with one foot stinky and soggy.

BIN JUICE

When I was done, I stood back and admired my artwork. It was pretty good, if I do say so myself. I reckoned Auntie GeeGee would've been proud of me.

I was so happy with it that part of me wanted everyone at school to know that I'd made it. For a split second I considered signing it with my own name, but I came to my senses pretty quickly when I realized I'd get detention till I was in my eighties if I ever got caught.

Instead, I finished it off with an 'AA' symbol that I'd been doodling in my notebook ever since I'd first had the idea of becoming an art superhero.

The AA logo looked much cooler than writing out 'Art Avenger' in full, and it added an extra layer of mystery to the whole thing.

I was the Art Avenger, my masterpiece was complete, and my sock was squelchy.

SOGGY SOCK

CHAPTER 7

THE STINK-PIPE BULLY

It was morning break before anyone noticed my painting, but when they did, they were like ants around a mouldy banana. There hadn't been this much excitement in the playground since Cindy Newman and Gretchen Heron got into a full-on fight over who liked their favourite rapper, Biggie Big, the most.

I'M THE BIGGEST BIGGIE BIG FAN!

I'M THE BIGGEST BIGGIE BIG FAN!

FIGHT! FIGHT! FIGHT! FIGHT!

To fully explain my artwork, first I need to tell you about the stink pipe. The stink pipe is this strange pipe that comes down the wall of the lower playground. No one knows what it's for but, judging by the smell coming from it, the pipe must be linked to the staffroom toilet, the canteen waste disposal AND the PE lost-property box.

I heard the reason why no one has seen Calvin Roberts since September is because he drank the water that comes out of the stink pipe and it dissolved all his internal organs. However, I have also heard that Calvin's family moved to Scotland, so you make your own mind up.

For my masterpiece, I painted a genie-ghost thing coming out of the stink pipe with the words 'BULLYING STINKS' above it. Anyone with half a brain could see that the stink-pipe bully was supposed to be Rory.

For the rest of the week all anyone could talk about was my painting. Everyone had started calling it *The Stink-pipe Bully* and it quickly got shortened to the SPB.

DID YOU SEE THE SPB?

IT'S AWESOME!

YEAH!

WHO D'YA THINK DID IT?

Nobody flat out called Rory the SPB to his face, but he knew it and everyone else knew it. I can't 100 per cent say that my painting caused Rory to be any less of a bully, but I'm pretty sure it did penetrate his man-sized skull and get through to his boy-sized brain just a little bit.

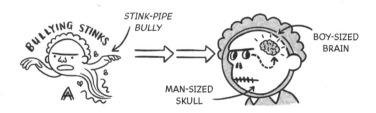

STINK-PIPE BULLY

BULLYING STINKS

A

MAN-SIZED SKULL

BOY-SIZED BRAIN

I might be imagining it, but I swear Rory has actually started being slightly nicer — or at least a little less nasty — to everyone. If there was a scientific measurement for bullying, Rory's graph would show a gradual decline directly after the SPB incident. And, you know what, I'm taking that as a win.

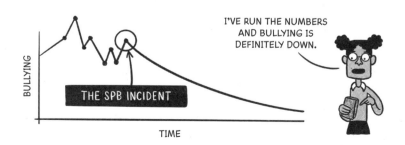

I'VE RUN THE NUMBERS AND BULLYING IS DEFINITELY DOWN.

BULLYING

THE SPB INCIDENT

TIME

The only thing that I really regretted was not signing my work 'Art Avenger' in full. Nobody knew what 'AA' stood for. Anish Akbar was the prime suspect — he got summoned to Mrs McGovern's office for a grilling. She quickly worked out it couldn't have been him though — if you'd ever seen the drawing Anish did of his family you'd know why. Apparently his dad is bigger than his house!

MY FAMILY BY ANISH AKBAR, AGED 12

It felt really good to have done something that everyone was talking about, but it really frustrated me that no one knew I'd made it. I always knew that I wouldn't be able to get the credit for it as Trixie, but I'd at least hoped the Art Avenger might become playground famous.

The question on everyone's lips at school that week was: 'Just who is AA?' There were a few other suspects but none of them seemed to fit. Only I knew the truth.

AA: THE MAIN SUSPECTS

ASHLEY ADAMS	ANNE ABBOT	ADEBAYO AKINFENWA	AN AARDVARK
FROM YEAR 11	DINNER LADY	LOCAL RUGBY PLAYER	FROM THE ZOO

I decided that next time (if there was a next time) I'd definitely be signing my name in full.

. . . .

GERALDINE PUFFIN

Geraldine Puffin here. There blooming well better be a next time, otherwise this is going to be one stupidly short book!

75

CHAPTER 8

BLAMMO!

I was still buzzing from my first-ever Art Avenger mission. The adrenalin rush I got when I was painting was like riding one of the roller coasters they reject for being too dangerous.

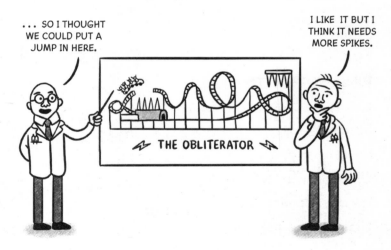

... SO I THOUGHT WE COULD PUT A JUMP IN HERE.

I LIKE IT BUT I THINK IT NEEDS MORE SPIKES.

⚡ THE OBLITERATOR ⚡

Rory wasn't exactly a saint, but he was definitely being a lot nicer. He was at the stage where he would still knock your books out of your hands, but he'd also help you pick them up again afterwards.

Overall, I decided to call it a success — in school terms, a B+. (Or, if Mrs Harris was marking it, a B- because she still hates me from the 'cloned teachers but without the coffee breath' comic.) Despite being on a high and itching to tell someone, I kept quiet and channelled all my artistic energy into a new comic I was making called *Blammo*.

CHILDREN'S AUTHOR

MY NEW BOOK

When I was in Year 6, a children's author did an assembly at my old school. He said he'd started out when he was a kid by making his own comics and selling them in the playground.

The comics he showed us were pretty rubbish, so I reckoned it wouldn't be too difficult for me to make some sweet cash by selling copies of *Blammo*.

SO THIS WAS MY FIRST-EVER COMIC, *SUPER FRIENDLY FRIENDS*.

THAT SUCKS. I COULD DO MUCH BETTER.

I already had loads of comic-strip ideas of my own, but the art book Miss Handley had given me inspired a new one. I called it 'Not-Very-Clever Aliens' and it was basically about these stupid aliens doing really stupid stuff. The idea came from an artist called Keith Haring, who drew lots of funny outline people.

NOT–VERY–CLEVER ALIENS

WHY ARE YOU DANCING ROUND THE PLANT POT?

I HEARD IT MAKES THE SEED GROW QUICKER

WHAT ARE YOU GROWING?

CHICKEN!
FRESH EGGS

FACT FILE:
KEITH HARING

He was an American pop artist.

His art is inspired by the cartoons he watched as a child.

He used to graffiti on the New York subway.

He was famous for drawing colourful outline characters.

He used chalk instead of spray paint.

He often got into trouble with the police.

He also drew UFOs, aliens, babies and barking dogs.

He was a big fan of hip-hop music.

I figured that two heads were definitely better than one as far as my *Blammo* business enterprise was concerned, so I invited Beeks over to help out. The way I saw it, Beeks could draw a few of the comic strips and help me sell *Blammo* in the playground. In return, I would cut him in on a slice of the profits.

Me and Beeks have history when it comes to being business partners. When I was losing my milk teeth, we came up with an almost foolproof way to scam the tooth fairies.

LISTEN UP, I'VE GOT A FOOLPROOF PLAN . . .

UH HUH.

The tooth fairy who went to Beeks's house
gave him £3 per tooth, but my tooth fairy was
a lot stingier and only gave me £1.

I worked out that, if I gave my teeth to Beeks
to put under his pillow, he could give me £2 and
keep £1 for himself and we'd still both be up on
the deal.

The plan definitely would've been foolproof if
only we hadn't got greedy and started letting
other kids from school in on it.

I've always wondered why the tooth fairy is the only magical creature dedicated to collecting waste body parts. Why isn't there a scab goblin, a toenail elf or an earwax pixie?

Just as Beeks was telling me about an idea he'd had for a comic strip based on his 'get in the bin' catchphrase, Mum barged into my room waving a copy of the *Wormwood Post*. She told us to look at the front page. There was a story about a boy who had been knocked over by a car just outside school.

BOY KNOCKED DOWN OUTSIDE SCHOOL

WORMWOOD HIGH PUPIL HIT BY SPEEDING CAR

A 13-YEAR-OLD BOY IS SAID TO BE IN A STABLE CONDITION AT WORMWOOD GENERAL HOSPITAL AFTER BEING INVOLVED IN AN ACCIDENT SHORTLY AFTER LEAVING SCHOOL YESTERDAY AFTERNOON. ACCORDING TO AN UNNAMED SOURCE, THE CAR THAT STRUCK DOWN THE YOUNGSTER WAS GOING WELL ABOVE THE SPEED LIMIT. A POLICE SPOKESMAN HAS STATED THAT A FULL INVESTIGATION WILL BE TAKING PLACE. MORE ON PAGE 3

JEREMIAH GOING, BUT WHAT SHOULD REPLACE HIM? MORE ON PAGE 11

Dad is always saying people drive like maniacs down that road.

Then, inside the paper, Mum showed us a competition to design a 'slow down' poster. She said we should quit drawing our silly comics and put our artistic talents to good use for once. My brain started to whirr into action.

Now, the cleverer ones among you are probably already one step ahead. I'm guessing you've spotted an opportunity for the Art Avenger to dust off his or her cape for a new mission. Well, the joke's on you as I don't wear a cape.

You're probably thinking that I entered the competition, my design won, Mum was proud of me, the cars slowed down and everything was

all jam sandwiches
and chocolate milk.

I'M SOOOO PROUD
OF YOU, DARLING.

And you could well be
right — there's only one
way to find out. (Spoiler
alert: that's not exactly
what happened. Plus I prefer banana milk.)

STOP TRYING
TO GUESS.

THE ONLY WAY TO
FIND OUT WHAT
HAPPENS IS TO
CARRY ON
READING.

BANANA
MILK

GERALDINE PUFFIN

*Geraldine Puffin here again.
I really think you should
consider a cape for your next
mission, Trixie. Have you
perhaps got an old shower
curtain you could use?*

CHAPTER 9

WARNING: THIS CHAPTER MAY CONTAIN DAD PANTS

Me and Beeks started working on a few ideas for a 'slow down' poster, but I got the feeling that the designs I was coming up with wouldn't be quite what the judges were looking for.

I didn't think my ideas would be good enough to enter in the competition, but when I saw the only idea Beeks had come up with I almost changed my mind.

After a while, Beeks's mum called him home for dinner so I decided to give up on the posters and draw some more 'Not-Very-Clever Aliens' comic strips for *Blammo* instead. As I flicked back through my art book to the Keith Haring page, another artist that Miss Handley had marked caught my eye.

FACT FILE:
ANTONY GORMLEY

He is a British sculptor.

A lot of his work is based on human figures.

His most famous work is the *Angel of the North*.

Local people call it 'Rusty Rita'.

It looks like a cross between a human and an aeroplane.

He placed 31 life-sized replicas of his own body on top of buildings around London.

He called it *Event Horizon*.

He made this sculpture called *Bed* out of 8,640 slices of bread.

For one artwork he filled a room with 35,000 small terracotta figures.

Antony Gormley is a sculptor who did this thing called *Event Horizon*. He made a load of statues based on himself and put them on the tops of buildings all around London. They looked so realistic that quite a few members of the public called the police saying they thought people were about to jump off buildings.

HE'S ON THE EDGE!

RELAX, MADAM, IT'S A SCULPTURE.

That gave me an idea that was even better than a 'slow down' poster.

First I needed to get hold of some supplies, including fluorescent yellow paint and a glue gun. The next day I went back to the art

I'VE JUST HAD AN IDEA THAT'S EVEN BETTER THAN DESIGNING A 'SLOW DOWN' POSTER.

department to see Miss Handley, and she let me 'borrow' whatever I needed. I might be paranoid but something she said made me think she was on to me.

HERE'S THE GLUE GUN. ARE YOU STICKING UP FOR YOUR CLASSMATES OR STICKING IT TO THE BULLIES?

ERR...

Even if Miss Handley had sussed that it was me who made *The Stink-pipe Bully*, I was still pretty confident she'd keep quiet. In my eyes, she had quickly become by far the coolest teacher in school. In fact, I wouldn't have been surprised if she wasn't actually a teacher at all and she'd lied in her interview.

...AND THIS CERTIFICATE PROVES I'M GENUINELY A REAL TEACHER AND I DEFINITELY DIDN'T JUST PRINT IT OFF AT HOME THIS MORNING OR ANYTHING.

On the way back home, I stopped at Hadderley's, which was in the middle of being refurbished.

Luckily there was still a huge skip filled with old mannequins round the back. There were arms, legs and bodies everywhere — it looked like the world's most painful game of Twister. I grabbed what I needed and headed home.

At home I rounded up a few more things: Mum's hairdryer, Travis's baseball cap and a stencil of my AA logo. I tied everything to my skateboard with a skipping rope and, under cover of darkness, I snuck out of the house.

My Art Avenger outfit made me almost invisible to the naked eye.

WOW! THAT SKATEBOARD FULL OF JUNK IS MOVING ALL BY ITSELF!

When I got to the road outside school, I started to assemble my Antony Gormley-inspired statue. I set the mannequin up and glued the hairdryer into its hands. I used the fluorescent paint to make it a high-vis vest and I stencilled an AA logo on its cap.

This time, though, I also wrote 'Art Avenger'
out in full on the back. If my plan worked,
I wanted everyone to know it was all down
to the Art Avenger.

As a final touch, I'd also brought a pair of Dad's
pants with me to cover up the smooth lump in
the mannequin's you-know-where region. (Don't
worry — I wore gloves for that bit.)

When I was finished I walked to the other end
of the road and, from a distance, it looked just
like a traffic-enforcement officer holding a
speed gun. I hoped drivers would think so too
and slow down when they saw it.

It looked pretty convincing to me. The question
was: would anyone else buy it?

CHAPTER 10

THIS CHAPTER DEFINITELY CONTAINS DAD PANTS

I didn't have to wait too long to find out if my mannequin was working.

I went to Beeks's after school the next day. He wanted to show me the comic strips he'd been working on for *Blammo*. I know you probably think that I've been quite mean to Beeks so far in this book but, to be honest, his 'Get in the Bin' comic strips were actually really good.

We were sitting drawing at Beeks's table with all our pens and pencils out when Beeks's dad, Mr O'Neal, came in. He jokingly asked if either of us was the Art Avenger.

I BET IT'S YOU, ISN'T IT, TRIXIE?

How did he know? I started to get a hot flush in my face — it was the same weird feeling you get when you think you might be in trouble. I asked Mr O'Neal what he meant and he told us all about this police-officer-scarecrow-type-thing (his words, not mine) that was slowing down the cars outside school. According to Mr O'Neal, it appeared overnight and everyone was talking about it. You can't imagine how awesome this was to hear. Not only was my Antony Gormley-inspired plan working but also, this time round, people were using the name 'Art Avenger'.

I knew I had to keep my excitement hidden, though, so I played it cool and showed Beeks a new comic strip I'd drawn called 'Bum-faced Snails'.

BUM-FACED SNAILS

About a week later, the success of my second secret mission was made official. I was in our kitchen making Triple Toast, one of my favourite after-school snacks, when Dad came in all stressed out.

He had to go to his work's bowling league that night and he couldn't find his lucky pants.

This whole 'lucky pants' thing was news to me but Mum filled me in on exactly what made them so lucky. Apparently the first time he wore them loads of good stuff happened. It was the day he got given his new company car, his football team won, he dropped his favourite mug and it bounced instead of breaking, and he bought a chocolate bar from the vending machine at work and two came out. Mum said he'd been wearing and washing them at least twice a week ever since, hoping to recapture

the magic of that first time.
In my defence, that amount
of wearing and washing
would explain why I
thought they were ready
for the bin or, more accurately, my mannequin.

In the end, Dad went bowling without his lucky
pants but if he'd stuck around for just five
more minutes, he would have seen them again.

Luckily for me,
he didn't. The
Wormwood Post
came through the
front door and
there they were:
Dad's pants smack
bang on the front
page. I couldn't
believe it.

LUCKY PANTS

WORMWOOD POST

MYSTERIOUS MANNEQUIN STOPS SPEEDING

JUST WHO IS THE ART AVENGER?

AND WHAT IS WITH THOSE PANTS?

AT SOME POINT YESTERDAY, A STRANGE SCULPTURE APPEARED ON WORMWOOD LANE AND OVERNIGHT THE NOTORIOUS ACCIDENT HOTSPOT HAS BECOME MUCH SAFER. THIS CURIOUS WORK OF ART HAS BEEN FOOLING MOTORISTS INTO SLOWING DOWN AND IS ALL THANKS TO SOMEBODY WHO CALLS THEMSELF THE 'ART AVENGER'. FULL STORY ON PAGE 3

'SLOW DOWN' POSTER CONTEST WINNER REVEALED INSIDE

Seeing the words 'Art Avenger' in black and white was a strange feeling. Strange but good. I started to get that same adrenalin buzz that I'd got when I was painting *The Stink-pipe Bully*.

I was brought down to earth, though, when I saw who had won the 'slow down' poster competition on page five.

Beeks had only gone and won it, and with a design that was suspiciously similar to one of my rejected ideas.

I didn't let it bother me too much though — I had some evidence that I needed to get rid of. If Mum or Dad saw the lucky pants on the front page, I would definitely be in hot water.

Let's just say that getting rid of evidence by eating it works a lot better in cartoons than in real life. I just got a really newspapery mouth — I ended up having to flush the evidence down the loo instead.

CHAPTER 11

BASKETBALL BEEF

I had successfully completed my second Art Avenger mission and this being-sort-of-famous thing was definitely something I could get used to. And, while I was hungry for more newspaper headlines, I wasn't LITERALLY hungry for them — give me Triple Toast any day of the week.

They say there is a fine line between genius and insanity and I'm pretty sure Beeks uses that line for tightrope practice.

To give you an example of what I call 'Beeks logic': he keeps hold of pens that have run out of ink so that he can 'use them to make mental notes'. He says his dream is to get all the colours in one of those four-colour pens to run out so that he can colour-code his mental notes.

IT'S MUM'S BIRTHDAY NEXT FRIDAY – LET ME MAKE A MENTAL NOTE OF THAT.

He has found a way to get double dinner helpings though, which I think is absolutely on the genius side of the line. Whenever his mum gives him Alphabetti spaghetti on toast, he also gets her to give him a tin of regular spaghetti. He tells her it's so he can 'underline the important bits'.

See what I mean? He's a mad genius!

I was round at Beeks's again to talk *Blammo* and something gave me the idea he was feeling guilty for copying my 'Slow down, you clown' idea.

The main giveaway was that, as soon as he saw me, he tried to hide the newspaper he was reading. (Great minds think alike!)

I told him not to worry — I'd already seen the paper and I was cool with it. The way I looked at it, I said, I was now entitled to half of whatever his prize was. He told me he'd been given a tub of those miniature-sized chocolate bars, which sounded great until I found out the only ones left were the coconut ones.

The coconut ones aren't exactly my favourite, but I suppose at least you get value for money with them. If you eat one during first break, you're still picking little bits out of your teeth come home time.

AHHH, COCONUT. THE GIFT THAT KEEPS ON GIVING.

One thing I've always wondered is: why are there so many chocolate bars with spacey-sounding names? There's Mars, Milky Way, Galaxy and Starbar, and I'm guessing there must be loads more still in development. If I worked in the product-development department at the chocolate-bar company, I'd suggest Uranus Chocolate Pieces just to see how far they got before anyone noticed.

THESE ARE DELIGHTFUL. WHAT DO YOU CALL THEM?

CHOCOLATE PIECES . . .

URANUS CHOCOLATE PIECES.

Beeks and me were all good, so we went outside to shoot some hoops. You'd think that because Beeks is tall, and he has a basketball hoop in his garden, he'd be the best player in school. Don't get me wrong — he's good, but Annika Tompkins is by far and away the best.

The problem was, at Wormwood, only boys were allowed to play basketball. The girls had to play netball instead. Beeks tried to get me on the team once but he got shouted down by the other boys.

I'd say that me, Annika Tompkins and Melissa Shah are all easily better than most boys. If it wasn't for Mr Bootle and his stupid rules we'd absolutely be on that team.

Mum said that, by not letting the girls play, Mr Bootle was 'cutting off his nose to spite his face' but I doubt he's able to find his nose among all that face fuzz.

The 'no girls' rule was so unfair, and the more I thought about it the angrier I got.

I started to get the beginnings of another Art Avenger idea. What I had in mind might not get me on the team, but it would definitely be fun to watch. I couldn't do it straight away though – I would have to wait till next week's big basketball game.

I picked up one of Beeks's old biros and made a mental note!

CHAPTER 12

SPENCER SMEDLEY

Spencer Smedley is the boy who all the girls in my class have a crush on, but I don't see the attraction myself.

HE'S SO DREAMY.

I FEEL FAINT.

The person who loves Spencer Smedley most, though, is Spencer Smedley himself. As my dad would say, 'If he was made of chocolate, he'd eat himself.'

NOT ONLY DO I LOOK AMAZING, I TASTE GREAT TOO.

He is completely obsessed with his hair too. He carries a comb in his back pocket and uses our classroom fish tank as a mirror. I swear those fish will need therapy later on in life.

SO, TELL ME, ARE YOU STILL HAVING NIGHTMARES ABOUT THE GIANT FACE WITH THE COMB?

Spencer also has super-rich parents who buy him anything he wants. His mum and dad are something called 'hedge-fund managers', which I'd never heard of and thought was a fancy name for people who trim your garden bushes. I even stuck up for them once when Dad said, 'People like the Smedleys are why the world is in such a mess right now.'

It turns out, though, that hedge-fund managers are actually something to do with banking. Knowing this doesn't stop me annoying Spencer by asking if his mum and dad can pop round sometime and take a look at our back garden.

To give you an idea of the kind of person Spencer is, his parents bought him a £200 pair of trainers once and he threw them away without wearing them because they were 'the wrong shade of blue'.

I WANTED A BLUEY BLUE, NOT A GREENY-BLUEY BLUE.

He also has this expensive talking watch imported from Japan. I'd ask for my money back if I were him, because none of the phrases seem to make much sense.

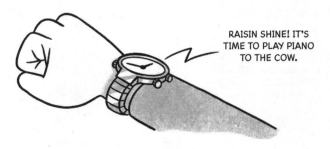

RAISIN SHINE! IT'S TIME TO PLAY PIANO TO THE COW.

We were in English and Mrs Krasinski was talking about characters from books and their fears. She went round the class asking us all what we were afraid of, and I was the first one she asked. I didn't want anyone to know that I have a fear of bubble wrap so I lied and said I was scared of heights. If I'd known what some of the other kids' fears were, though, I wouldn't have bothered making something up.

When it came to Rory McGory's turn, Spencer butted in before Rory got a chance to speak.

I know Rory is a bully but Spencer's comment felt TOO mean. Especially as, ever since the *Stink-pipe Bully* incident, Rory had been a lot nicer to everyone. I almost kind of felt sorry for him.

Rory's shoes WERE falling apart but you couldn't really blame him. He lived with his nan and she couldn't afford to buy him new stuff all the time. (Although, according to Mum, Rory's nan spends all the money she DOES get for looking after him either at the bingo or on her dog — also called Bingo.)

Beeks was up next and was about to reveal his fear. If I'd been a gambling person, I would've put money on his fear being imaginary friends. When we were in preschool, Beeks imagined himself an imaginary friend who would jump out from places and scare him.

Well, it'd either be imaginary friends or the 'playing in the garden sprinkler naked' photo being made public, but I knew he'd 100 per cent be too embarrassed to even mention that.

Beeks was just about to speak when Spencer butted in again.

IF I WORE THOSE STUPID GLASSES, MY BIGGEST FEAR WOULD BE OWNING A MIRROR.

Beeks has always been self-conscious about his glasses, and I could tell Spencer's mean comment had cut deep.

All Mrs Krasinski did was the standard 'OK, settle down, class' and Spencer just sat there smirking. My blood was boiling!

That was it. Spencer Smedley had just put himself on the Art Avenger's hit list. It was time to get even — for Beeks, for Rory and for those poor traumatized goldfish.

CHAPTER 13

PICASS-HOL

Later that day, I sat in my room trying to come up with a way to teach Spencer Smedley a lesson. My brain had other ideas. It was preoccupied with random thoughts, like:

1) How come Dracula can't see his reflection in a mirror but he always has immaculate hair?

TO BE HONEST, I HAVEN'T GOT A CLUE, BUT I'M NOT COMPLAINING.

2) Do people ever mix up the World Wildlife Fund and World Wrestling Entertainment because their initials are so similar?

FOR THE LAST TIME, SIR, IT IS NOT OK TO BODY SLAM A PANDA.

The only way to get my brain back on track was to flick through the art book Miss Handley had given me. I landed on a page about an artist called Pablo Picasso, and inspiration struck.

Picasso is famous for making these weird portraits that make everyone's faces look like they've been cut into pieces and reassembled by a trained monkey — a trained monkey who isn't very good at jigsaw puzzles but does have a great sense of humour.

FACT FILE:
PABLO PICASSO

He was an abstract artist from Spain.

He helped invent an art style called cubism.

His portraits all look a bit strange.

HOW RUDE!

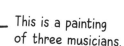

This is a painting of three musicians.

He didn't enjoy school and often got detention.

I decided to draw Spencer and give him the Picasso treatment. It was perfect. It was also imperfect. It was perfectly imperfect and Spencer was going to hate it!

But, once I had the picture, what was I going to do with it? I tried to think of something, but my brain started filling with more random thoughts.

3) Do crabs think that humans walk sideways?

4) How come only hurricanes and storms get given names? Why don't other types of weather get the same treatment?

I flicked back through my art book and this time I landed on an artist called Andy Warhol.

Andy Warhol was a pop artist who liked making pictures of everyday stuff, like cans of soup, bottles of Coke and old-fashioned celebrities, like the singer Elvis Presley. Once he had made a picture, he repeated it — lots and lots. One of his most famous works of art is a load of different versions of the olden-days actor Marilyn Monroe.

FACT FILE:
ANDY WARHOL

He was an American pop artist who had an art studio called The Factory.

WHO WANTS ART?

THE FACTORY

He loved to repeat his images.

He used to make prints of famous people and also ordinary things like soup cans and bottles of Coke.

This is an actor called Marilyn Monroe.

This is his Elvis Presley picture.

 He was a modern art superstar!

That's how I got the idea to make lots of copies of my Spencer Smedley portrait. A Picasso crossed with a Warhol — a Picass-hol?

The best thing was, I already knew how I was going to get the copies made, plus I knew exactly when to make them for maximum effect. I slipped my Picasso Spencer Smedley into my Top-Secret Documents folder and I let my brain go back into random mode.

CHAPTER 14

THE SWITCHEROO

For the last couple of weeks, way before I'd even thought about Art Avenging Spencer Smedley, me and Beeks had been staking out the school office. Originally we wanted to sneak on to the photocopier when Mrs Dewson's back was turned so that we could make copies of our first edition of *Blammo*.

11.02 A.M. MRS DEWSON FARTED – MAKE A NOTE OF THAT. IT COULD BE IMPORTANT.

ER, OK?

SKWEEE!

Now though, the intelligence we'd been gathering was going to be really useful for my mission to get back at Spencer.

I knew that, during first break every Wednesday, Mrs Dewson makes 800 copies of the Wormwood newsletter. A newsletter is then given to every child at afternoon register. She's like clockwork: she sets the copier going, then goes off to the staffroom and comes back about ten minutes later with a diet soup-in-a-cup. Mrs Dewson is a creature of habit and some of her habits are disgusting. These soups smell bad — like, really bad. Like a dog has been sick, eaten the sick, sicked the sick back up and then someone has microwaved it so it really hangs around in the air.

So there I was on Wednesday, hiding out in Mrs Dewson's office jungle. Mrs Dewson treats those plants like they're her kids — she has names for all of them.

JACQUELINE, YOU'RE LOOKING HEALTHY.

ARTHUR, HARRY, I HOPE YOU TWO HAVE MADE UP AND ARE FRIENDS AGAIN.

I waited for her to set the copier going and leave for the staffroom. As soon as she did, I took the Picasso Spencer Smedley out of my Top-Secret Documents folder and quickly swapped it for the newsletter, all the time keeping my eyes out for Mrs Dewson and my nose out for her soup.

As soon as the air filled with the smell of reheated double dog vomit, I whipped my artwork off the copier and put back the newsletter. Another Art Avenger success – this was getting easy. All I had to do now was wait till after lunch for the fallout.

I CAN'T WAIT TILL EVERYONE SEES THIS. SPENCER IS GOING TO BE SOOO MAD!

CHAPTER 15

THE FALLOUT

You usually risk a detention if you don't get to afternoon register on time, but this was worth it. I wanted to savour the sound of laughter filling the hallway. And I wasn't disappointed.

It was like the time Mrs Hollingsworth came out of the staffroom toilet with the back of her skirt tucked into her knickers.

You kind of lose all authority when your pants are on public display.

As I walked down the corridor, I could hear laughter coming out of every classroom. When I got to my class, everyone was cracking up. I could see Spencer sitting with his head in his hands.

It looked like he was crying, but when I got closer I could see he was actually crying with laughter. I didn't understand — he was supposed to be insulted by all the Picasso portraits.

It took a while for the penny to drop but, when I saw what everyone was actually laughing at, I wanted the ground to swallow me up.

It was the 'playing in the garden sprinkler naked' photo! It had somehow got stuck to the Picasso Spencer Smedley when they were inside my Top-Secret Documents folder. I had accidentally photocopied the most embarrassing picture of me in existence and distributed it across the school.

This was bad. This was very bad. This was worse than 'putting both legs in one pant hole, knocking yourself unconscious, waking up and asking your grandma if you can ride the teacups again' levels of bad. Now I knew how Mrs Hollingsworth must have felt when she showed her knickers to the whole school.

Everyone was laughing at me and Beeks. It was the exact opposite of what was supposed to happen.

BEEKS?
BUTTCHEEKS
MORE LIKE!

It took a while for the whole naked-sprinkler-photo thing to die down. I think, in the end, everyone at school must have seen that picture.

On the plus side, at least no one could possibly suspect me of being the Art Avenger. I mean, who on earth would do that to themselves on purpose?

CHAPTER 16

BOUNCING BACK

I had suffered my first Art Avenger fail. I bet Banksy has never sent a naked picture of himself to everyone he knows. He is probably far too busy counting all his money and having his work adored by millions. That is the dream — imagine having your work on display for everyone to admire. I wouldn't complain about having his money either!

I SIMPLY MUST BUY THIS SCULPTURE FOR TEN MILLION POUNDS.

I decided the best thing to do was concentrate on my basketball plan.

Before every big basketball match, Mr James, the caretaker, re-marks the lines of the court. And he always makes the same joke when he wheels the court marker to the sports hall.

MAKE WAY! REMARKABLE PERSON COMING THROUGH. GET IT? BECAUSE I'M ...

... RE-MARKING THE BASKETBALL COURT.

My plan was simple and, if you've been paying attention to the artist fact files, you might already know what I was going to do. (If you haven't got a clue what I'm on about, go back and reread the fact file about Bridget Riley on page 58.)

I was going to give the basketball court a Bridget Riley-style makeover.

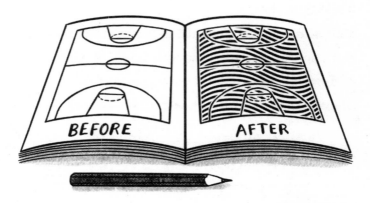

First, I needed to go to the art department and get a few things from Miss Handley – Wormwood's best-ever teacher. When I got there, she was sitting and drawing something in her sketch pad. When I said 'hi' she nearly jumped out of her skin.

It was the same reaction that Dad had when I caught him gluing one of Mum's good plates back together.

I got some white and black paint and a few paint rollers, no questions asked. In fact, as I was leaving, Miss Handley asked me if I wanted to try out some new glow-in-the-dark paint she'd just got in. I immediately started to think of the possibilities. I wasn't sure how or why, but I had a feeling it might come in useful.

After school, I got all my equipment together and put on my Art Avenger outfit. I told Mum that I'd be doing an art project round at Beeks's, so only really half a lie. I also borrowed Dad's head torch for the mission. He wouldn't miss it – he only ever uses it when there's a power cut or he's doing his X-Men impression.

I also took some super-strong duct tape with me, plus our broom handle, our mop handle and our garden-rake handle.

When I climbed through the school fence, the General was lying by his kennel looking depressed as usual. I guess I'd be miserable too if the place I slept in was dark and dingy and smelled a bit funky. I reckon that must be why Travis is always in such a bad mood. You'd think Mr James would give the kennel a lick of paint.

Anyway, I had a present for the General. For Christmas, Dad got a subscription to 'Cured Meats of the World by Post', which means he gets sent dried sausages from different countries every month. That month, the sausages were from Albania, and they were definitely the smelliest ones yet. (Dad chews on these foul-smelling sticks of meat while we're trying to watch TV and it's gross.)

THAT IS DISGUSTING!

I'd figured I'd be killing two birds with one stone by a) getting the sausages out of our house, and b) giving the General a little treat. The General chewed the Albanian sausage for a bit, then spat it out and walked away in disgust. It's official: my dad is less fussy than an old, depressed dog.

HYUK!

I could see the light in the sports hall was still on — Mr James hadn't finished re-marking the court yet. I wasn't too late.

AND

IIIᵢᵢᵢ - EEEₑₑ - IIIᴵᴵᴵ...

When Mr James finally came out, I snuck in behind him just as the door was closing.

I was able to do this without being heard thanks to two things.

Firstly, the sports-hall door closed very, very slowly and made a sound like Chewbacca treading on Lego.

Secondly, Mr James had his headphones on and he was singing very, very loudly and very badly (either that or he had trodden on Lego too).

I switched on the head torch and got to work. I'd once seen a cartoon of a kid who was given lines as punishment, and to make it quicker he tied three pens together – I was basically doing the same thing but on a much bigger scale.

It took me a couple of hours to finish my Bridget Riley basketball-court makeover, but it was going to be worth it. When I was done, I cranked up the thermostat so the paint would dry in time, then I headed for home.

As I passed the General's kennel on the way out, I noticed how clear the night sky was that evening. The bright stars reminded me of something I'd seen in my art book and gave me an idea for a bonus Art Avenger mission. As I stood there, looking at the full moon, I heard what sounded like the howl of a werewolf – although it could well have been Mr James belting out a power ballad.

Then it was home to rest – I had a big day of revenge ahead of me. Mr Bootle and the boys wouldn't let us girls play basketball and BOY were they going to regret it.

CHAPTER 17

BARF-SKETBALL

Everybody at school was at the game.
Wormwood were playing against Sir John Percy's
all-boys school. Sir John Percy's were like a
team of robots — they all had identical haircuts
and matching tracksuits. As they jogged on to
the court, they did this chant that I think was
supposed to intimidate their opponents.

ATTACK, ATTACK, SHOW NO MERCY – WE ARE
THE BOYS FROM SIR JOHN PERCY.

Everyone was talking about the new court design. I think Mr James must have been weirded out when he first saw it, but Mrs McGovern seemed to really like it so he kept quiet and took the praise.

Beeks came and sat next to me with the rest of the spectators – he wasn't playing and he didn't seem too happy about it. He said he swore he'd packed his trainers that morning but he couldn't find them anywhere. What he didn't know was, it was me who had hidden them.

Beeks could be annoying sometimes, but, if my plan was going to go the way I hoped it would, I really didn't want him out there on that court. He is my best friend after all, plus he's the ONLY one of the boys who stuck up for us girls.

There was a part of me that had been thinking of telling Beeks all about the Art Avenger. I thought it would be kind of nice to have someone to share my secret with but, the way I figured it, the more people who knew, the more likely I was to get caught. Besides, doing everything on my own had much more of a superhero vibe about it. I was a lone wolf, righting wrongs and fighting injustices using

the power of art. For now, it was just me
against the world, or, more accurately, me
against the Wormwood High basketball team.

Spencer was captain in Beeks's absence and he
made sure this fact was known to everyone.

To be honest, after the first five minutes I
started to have doubts that my Bridget Riley
basketball-court makeover was going to have
the desired effect. I was hoping that, at the
very least, it would make the boys feel a bit
wobbly and maybe fall over a few times.
Nothing was happening, though, and I was
beginning to think all my efforts were for

nothing. Then, towards the end of the first quarter, I felt a glimmer of hope when Dudley Davis missed an easy catch.

The second quarter was when it all started to really go wrong (or right, depending on your point of view). It looked like the teams were playing on a moving ship — legs were wobbling, people were losing the ability to throw and catch, and then Tristan Patel started a chain reaction that would go down in Wormwood High School history.

He came over to the subs bench, saying he was going to be sick. Mr Bootle shouted at him to stop being silly.

Tristan did not follow this order. Instead, he started to barf. To make matters worse, he tried to hold the sick in by putting his hands over his mouth. This only served to create a sprinkler effect, and he sprayed Mr Bootle and half the subs bench with chunder.

Dudley Davis was next to blow chunks — it was projectile and pretty darn impressive. He looked like one of those little statues that they have in fancy water fountains.

They say that yawning is contagious. I can't comment on that but I know for 100 per cent certain that barfing definitely is. After Dudley had erupted, Brian Solanke spewed directly on Spencer Smedley's face.

This in turn made Spencer be sick all over himself. I don't think his fancy Japanese watch was particularly impressed.

Everybody in the crowd was in hysterics. Spencer tried to run away in shame, but one of the Sir John Percy's robots vomited in his path, creating the world's grossest Slip 'N' Slide.

After that it was pretty much a free-for-all —
there was not a boy on that court who hadn't
either been sick or been covered in sick. It
was Spewmageddon!

Annika Tompkins, Melissa Shah and the rest
of the girls who weren't allowed to be on the
basketball team were loving it.

One thing I remember feeling glad about was the fact I'd remembered to turn the thermostat back down before the game. I don't even want to think about how bad it would've smelled in that sports hall if I hadn't — although that is now what I'm thinking about. I'm guessing it would've smelled worse than one of Mrs Dewson's diet soup-in-a-cups being stirred with an Albanian sausage.

The aim of this Art Avenger mission was supposed to just be sweet, sweet revenge, but there was an additional, unplanned upside. The PE teachers quickly rescheduled the match for the next day at Sir John Percy's. And, because all the boys were off sick, Mr Bootle was forced to let us girls play.

Beeks was back as captain and he led us to a thumping victory — Wormwood's first-ever win over Sir John Percy's.

All in all, a brilliant result. Spencer and Mr Bootle had suffered Spewmageddon, the girls were finally on the basketball team, and the Art Avenger was back on track!

CHAPTER 18

SHARING MY SECRET

A few days later, I went round to Beeks's house after school again to put the final touches on our first edition of *Blammo*. I just needed a few more of Beeks's 'Get in the Bin' comic strips and then we'd be ready to make some copies.

I wasn't going to mess up with the photocopier this time round – I'd have Beeks with me on lookout duty.

Having said that, the last time Beeks was my lookout, things didn't exactly go off without a hitch. A few summers ago, we planned to 'liberate' a few apples from Mr Grimes's apple tree.

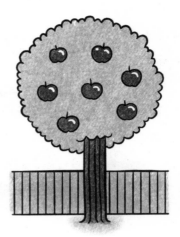

Geraldine Puffin here. I in no way endorse the act of stealing apples so please don't do it.

GERALDINE PUFFIN

Hang on a minute, darling, didn't you 'borrow' some rosemary from next door's herb garden last week?

GERALD PUFFIN

Ermmm, I don't remember that at all. How about we just carry on with the apple-stealing story?

GERALDINE PUFFIN

Mr Grimes lives in the house between my house and Beeks's, and every morning at eleven he goes to buy a newspaper. This gave us about a twenty-minute window to go into his garden and grab as many apples as we could.

I'm not even sure why we were doing it because I don't really like apples all that much. I got put off when I bit into one once and there was a maggot inside it. Dad told me it probably wasn't a maggot; it was most likely a moth larva — this didn't make the situation any better.

WELL, TECHNICALLY IT'S A MOTH LARVA.

I guess we were just stealing apples for something fun to do because the summer holidays can drag. The plan was that I would climb up the apple tree and Beeks would stand on lookout in the alley that goes from the street to the garden. We agreed that, so as not to raise suspicion, when Beeks saw Mr Grimes coming he would make a bird noise. The only problem was the bird that Beeks chose was a talking parrot.

SQUAWK... HURRY UP WITH THOSE APPLES, TRIXIE... SQUAWK... MR GRIMES IS BACK FROM THE SHOP... SQUAWK... GET OUT OF MR GRIMES'S GARDEN, TRIXIE... SQUAWK!

Instead of warning me, he dropped me right in it.

I thought we would be all right getting the copies of *Blammo* made, just as long as bird calls weren't a major part of the plan!

I tried to show Beeks a new comic strip I'd come up with called 'Barry Plopper', about a boy wizard whose magic spells didn't exactly work, but Beeks was more interested in talking about the basketball rematch and the chunderfest.

After Mr James had mopped down the court with super-strong disinfectant for about the twentieth time, he spotted the Art Avenger logo I'd hidden in the corner.

Everyone in school was suddenly obsessed with the Art Avenger again, and they all had their own theories about who was behind it.

I THINK THE ART AVENGER IS ACTUALLY A TOP-SECRET GOVERNMENT PLAN TO GET MORE KIDS INTO ART.

I THINK IT'S DERRICK FLETCHER FROM YEAR 10.

Beeks kept saying that whoever HE was, HE must be someone really cool. I really wanted to tell Beeks that it wasn't a HE — it was a ME! I've known Beeks for, like, forever and, despite us having our ups and downs, I decided it was finally time he knew about my secret identity. I plucked up the courage and just spat it out.

I KNOW YOU'RE NOT GOING TO BELIEVE THIS BUT . . .

IT'S ME.

I'M THE ART AVENGER.

Beeks started rolling on the floor laughing out loud. This was an actual real-life ROFLOL. It was clearly his 'I don't believe you — how on earth could YOU be the Art Avenger?' ROFLOL. He followed it up with several shouts of 'Get in the bin!' so I definitely needed to convince him.

After he was done with all the ROFLOLing and the get-in-the-binning, I showed him that I could draw the AA logo perfectly. But he said that proved nothing and that everyone at school could draw it. He showed me the back of his maths book — it was covered in hundreds of AAs.

He actually told me that HE was more likely to be the Art Avenger than I was!

Half of me was a bit disappointed that Beeks didn't believe me, but the other half thought it was probably for the best. After all, I'd got this far on my own. I went back home with our first edition of *Blammo* and left Beeks listing people he thought the Art Avenger could be.

MY MONEY IS ON CHAD GIBSON – ALTHOUGH I DID HEAR THE ART AVENGER COULD BE A TOP-SECRET GOVERNMENT PLAN TO GET MORE KIDS INTO ART.

EITHER THAT OR DERRICK FLETCHER FROM YEAR 10.

CHAPTER 19

GET IN THE BIN

You'll be glad to know that Beeks and me managed to get twenty-six copies of *Blammo* photocopied without the need for any parrot impressions.

We were planning to sell them in the playground at lunchtime so we needed something to stand on.

Beeks found a crate round the back of the canteen that would do the job. I'm not sure what the crate had been used for, but it stank of milk that had been left out in the sun for too long.

I'm not gonna lie: business was slow. After we'd been on the crate for fifteen minutes, we'd only sold one copy to Dudley. It didn't help that Derren Devlin was selling chocolate bars from his rucksack and stealing our potential customers.

Things did pick up a bit when Derren got busted by the dinner ladies, although I think my decision to ditch the crate also helped. You can't blame people for not wanting to buy a comic from a shop that smells of sour cheese.

But, with twenty minutes of lunchtime left, we'd still only sold five copies. Then Beeks had a rare flash of inspiration.

I'M HAVING A RARE FLASH OF INSPIRATION.

He got a red pen out of his bag and drew the AA logo on the cover of every *Blammo*.

As soon as he started shouting out that they were 'special, ultra-rare-edition comics signed by the Art Avenger' everyone in the playground wanted one.

I guess we must have been too popular though, because we attracted the attention of Mr Chippenham, which, trust me, was not a good thing. Mr Chippenham is the teacher who all the kids are scared of.

WHAT'S GOING ON HERE? PICKLE! O'NEAL! HAND THOSE OVER.

There's a rumour that Mr Chippenham locks children in his stationery cupboard to punish them and, once, he locked a kid in there on the last day of term and completely forgot about him. They say the boy's skeleton was found on the first day back after summer.

Everyone says that the reason he's so angry is because his wife left him for someone far less miserable. (I know, I know — that doesn't narrow it down much.)

PEOPLE LESS MISERABLE THAN MR CHIPPENHAM

I think the fact he always gets turned down for the deputy-head job whenever it comes up is also a big factor in his bitterness. I don't think you can blame the hiring committee though — especially if that skeleton-in-the-cupboard thing is true.

All teachers, no matter how angry or dead behind the eyes, have one thing that they are really passionate about. If you can find out what that one thing is and start them off talking about it, you're on easy street. We used to have competitions to see how much of the lesson we could get each teacher to talk for. With Mr Chippenham, that one thing was his car, and if you got the questioning just right you could waste a good half hour.

TELL US ABOUT YOUR CAR, SIR.

I LOVE THE BROWN COLOUR.

WELL, TECHNICALLY IT'S CINNAMON — OF COURSE IT WAS SAHARA BEIGE WHEN I FIRST BOUGHT IT. THAT WAS WAY BACK IN 1978 . . .

Back to the playground – Mr Chippenham grabbed our *Blammos* and read out the names of the cartoons in a high-pitched, sarcastic voice.

When he got to Beeks's 'Get in the Bin' comic, he said:

All our hard work, ridiculed and destroyed. This was definitely a case for the Art Avenger, but what could I do? The obvious way to get back at Mr Chippenham was to do something to his car.

I ruled that out, though, because if I got caught I'd definitely be in a world of trouble.

People get funny about their cars. I found that out last year after I gave Dad's car a wash and wax. How was I supposed to know that the 'wax' part of 'wash and wax' doesn't mean 'do a cool design on it with wax crayons'?

No, I was going to have to approach this problem from a slightly different angle.

CHAPTER 20

DUNG, DUNG, DUNG!

What do you do if you see a spaceman?

Park in it, man!

That is possibly the only joke in existence about parking spaces. You'll see why I just told you it if you carry on reading.

Along with the headmistress and the deputy head, Mr Chippenham is the only other member of staff who has their own dedicated car-parking spot.

RESERVED FOR

MR CHIPPENHAM

I think they gave it to him to stop him getting angry about constantly missing out on the deputy-head job. (If that's the case, though, it's not working very well.)

He loves that parking space almost as much as he loves his car. You'll often see him spitting on a hanky and polishing the name plaque.

Sometimes he brings in his own brush from home so he can give it a sweep.

THERE YOU GO, MATILDA. DOES THAT FEEL GOOD?

MR CHIPPENHAM

Every now and then, he even parks his car in the space next to it, just to give his own parking space a rest!

So the car-parking space was definitely going to be my target — I just needed to work out what to do to it. I flicked through Miss Handley's art book for inspiration, and I was about to give up when I found this guy:

FACT FILE:
CHRIS OFILI

He was born in Britain and his parents were from Nigeria.

He was the first black artist to win the Turner Prize.

IMPORTANT ART PRIZE

He uses a lot of elephant dung in his artwork.

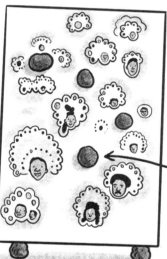

Sometimes he sticks it on to his canvases.

Sometimes he stands his pictures on blobs of elephant poo.

He is inspired by hip-hop and jazz music.

He includes pictures of famous black musicians in his art.

Filling Mr Chippenham's space with elephant dung sounded like a great idea, but this was Wormwood and I couldn't exactly get elephant dung from the corner shop.

TWO PACKS OF FOOTBALL STICKERS AND HALF A TON OF ELEPHANT DUNG, PLEASE.

I looked out of my bedroom window and the answer hit me right between the eyes. Not literally though, because the answer was horse manure. Having that hit you right between the eyes would be pretty gross.

Mr Grimes has a big, steaming pile of horse manure in his garden that he uses on his vegetable patch.

He sometimes comes round and offers Mum some of his runner beans or leeks. Now, vegetables aren't exactly my cup of tea at the best of times, but I'm definitely not going to eat vegetables that have spent their lives covered in horse poo.

If I ever have my window open when the wind is blowing in the wrong direction, his manure pile makes my bedroom smell just like Travis's.

My plan was simple: as soon as Mr Grimes sat down to watch TV, I'd sneak out with a wheelbarrow of horse poo, take it to school and dump it on Mr Chippenham's parking space.

I think Mr Grimes must be a bit deaf. His TV is always so loud that everyone in our house can hear when he starts watching his game shows.

I was in my Art Avenger outfit with my ear against the wall, waiting to hear the theme tune to *Cash Bang Wallop* or *Millionairheads*.

WELCOME TO ANOTHER EPISODE OF *MIND YOUR OWN QUIZNESS*!

As soon as I was sure that Mr Grimes was distracted, I headed to school with a wheelbarrow full to the brim of icky-smelling foulness topped with a tiny Art Avenger flag. I also took the glow-in-the-dark paint with me. If I had enough time, I would fit in a bonus Art Avenger mission.

Mr Chippenham was going to pay for ripping up *Blammo* and publicly ridiculing me and Beeks. Or, should I say, his car-parking space was!

CHAPTER 21

A WHEELIE BIG SURPRISE

I swear that wheelbarrow must have been
older than Mr Grimes himself. It was more rust
than metal, and it made noises like my dad does
when he gets out of a chair.

EEEEEEEEEEEEE

I'd just managed to squeeze the wheelbarrow full
of poo through the gap in the fence, and I was
almost at the car park, when I heard a crack.

Like the most talented member of a boy band, the wheel had decided to leave the rest of the wheelbarrow behind and go solo.

I quickly caught up with the wheel, which had made a break for it, and then reunited it with the rest of the band. I was on my knees, trying to fix it back in place, when I heard . . .

I picked up the handles of the wheelbarrow and started to run. The only problem was, my legs were moving but the wheel-less wheelbarrow (barrow?) wasn't. I looked like one of those cartoon characters that runs on the spot for a split second before racing off. Only I didn't race off – I went over the top of the barrow

and fell head first into the disgusting mountain
of manure.

As I wiped the grossness from my eyes, things
got even worse . . . It was Rory McGory.

Of all the people to discover my true identity,
it had to be him. I guessed he was still angry
about the whole stink-pipe thing.

He said that he had 'been looking forward to this moment for a while now'. I thought I was definitely getting a pummelling, or a turbo noogie at the very least, but then something really weird happened. Rory said:

He explained that seeing my *Stink-pipe Bully* painting had been the wake-up call he needed. He'd realized that when he was actually nice to people, people were nice back, and it was all thanks to the Art Avenger. For the first time since he'd been at Wormwood, he had friends. Rory started to tell me about how unhappy he was living with his nan, and how he guessed he had been taking it out on his classmates.

But all this was quickly followed by a punch to my arm, and he said:

After that, Rory helped me fix the wheel back on to the barrow and we carried on with the mission together. We dumped the manure in Mr Chippenham's parking space and Rory stuck the Art Avenger flag on top of the heap.

It looked a bit like one of those signs that they stick in the ice cream at posh cafes so

you can tell what the different flavours are.
This was definitely not rum and raisin though.
(Having said that, I suppose there could well
have been raisins in there. I'm not 100 per cent
sure what horses eat.)

ERRR,
I DON'T EAT
RAISINS BUT
I AM PARTIAL
TO A DROP
OF RUM.

As we headed back towards the gap in the
fence, I told Rory I had a bonus Art Avenger
mission to complete and that HE was going to
help me.

I explained to Rory that the horse poo in
Mr Chippenham's parking space had purely been
about revenge, so I needed to do something
good to rebalance my karma. And that's exactly
what we did next.

CHAPTER 22

THE BONUS ART AVENGER MISSION

What I'm going to tell you about in this chapter sort of started a while ago now, and you might not remember everything. Especially if you aren't reading this book all in one go. To be honest, I tend not to read books all in one go, mainly because I get easily distrac— Ooh, look! A butterfly!

LOOK AT ME!
LOOK AT ME!

Don't worry. I had to do a quick recap for Rory's benefit, so you may as well listen in too.

OK, so, back in chapter something-or-other I tried to cheer up the General (aka the world's most depressed dog) by giving him one of my dad's dried sausages. He wasn't impressed and to be honest I don't blame him.

EVEN I FIND THAT DISGUSTING, AND I'VE CHEWED A P.E. TEACHER'S FLIP-FLOP.

But do you remember when I was coming back from my basketball-court-makeover mission that I said the stars above the General's kennel reminded me of something I'd seen in my art book? Well, that thing was a painting called *The Starry Night* by an artist you might have heard of called Vincent van Gogh.

FACT FILE:
VINCENT VAN GOGH

He is one of the most famous artists of all time.

He painted sunflowers <u>A LOT!</u>

His art style is called post-impressionism.

He made loads of paintings of his bedroom.

You can see all the individual brush marks in his paintings.

He cut off his own ear.

The Starry Night is one of his most well-known paintings

The two things that most people know about Vincent van Gogh are that he used to paint sunflowers a lot and also that he chopped one of his ears off. Not sure why he did that — I can only assume his parents must have nagged him worse than mine nag me.

TIDY YOUR ROOM, VINCENT.

WELL, THERE'S ONLY ONE THING FOR IT.

Anyway, that painting, the sad dog and the glow-in-the-dark paint that Miss Handley had given me had all been mixing around in my head for some time now. (Not literally. That would just be weird.) And that's how I came up with the idea to give the General's kennel a *Starry Night* facelift.

Glo Glo

I showed Rory a sketch I'd made and we got to work with the glow-in-the-dark paint.

I couldn't tell whether the General liked it or not, but he was definitely mesmerized. He had exactly the kind of expression you'd expect from a dog looking at one of the world's most famous paintings being recreated on their kennel using glow-in-the-dark paint.

When we were done, the General came running towards me with his tail wagging. It was the most I'd ever seen him move. He jumped up and started licking the remaining bits of horse manure off my face. I guess it must have been dog for 'thank you'.

I was glad that he liked what we'd done to his kennel, but the licking was gross, for two reasons. Firstly, EWWWWW, eating horse manure — that is just grim! Secondly, on the scale of things that this dog would rather eat, horse poo ranked higher than my dad's dried sausages. That fact is all I'll be able to think about the next time I see Dad chewing on one of his sausage sticks from Slovakia.

CHAPTER 23

CHIPPENHAM INVESTIGATES!

The next day at school, Mr Chippenham was fuming about the manure in his parking space.

THIS IS A COMPLETE OUTRAGE!

THE CULPRIT WILL BE PUNISHED!

He turned his stationery cupboard into an interrogation room and called kids in one by one to find out what they knew. The Art Avenger was already Wormwood High's most wanted after the basketball-court stunt but this was another level.

I was worried at first, but then I realized he was only grilling the usual troublemakers. Rory got called in last, but I was pretty confident he wasn't going to say anything.

Well, I WAS pretty confident until, straight after Rory came out, MY name got called. I couldn't believe he'd ratted me out!

Rory winked at me as I walked past him on my way to the investigation cupboard.

Before I could blurt out that Rory was a liar, Mr Chippenham said:

AS YOU'RE A FELLOW VICTIM OF THIS ART AVENGER CHARACTER, TRIXIE, I WANT TO ASSURE YOU I WILL BE DOING EVERYTHING IN MY POWER TO CATCH HIM.

My 'playing in the garden sprinkler naked' photocopier mix-up had actually helped me out (although I was STILL a bit annoyed that everyone kept assuming the Art Avenger was a HIM!).

Mr Chippenham also set up an anonymous tip-off box, where kids could post who they thought the Art Avenger was, but this quickly got abused.

Back in maths class, it wasn't long before Rory
was back to his bad ways. I find maths really
tricky but luckily I sit next to the human
calculator, Suranna Adebayo. The good thing
about sitting next to Suranna Adebayo is that
she has this habit of staring up at the ceiling
when she's working out a problem. This makes
it really easy to sneak a peek at her answers.

She's brilliant at maths but not brilliant at hiding her work.

Halfway through learning about the angles of different triangles, I got hit on the back of the head by a screwed-up ball of paper. I turned round to give Rory evils but, before I could, he whispered at me to open it up.

I wasn't falling for that one but Rory whispered slightly louder . . .

JUST OPEN IT UP.
IT'S NOT A TRICK –
100 PER CENT HONEST.

Later on in the playground, Rory came up to me.

DID YOU LIKE THAT? I THOUGHT YOUR ARTY FRIEND MIGHT WANT TO ENTER.

WHY DID YOU SCREW IT UP AND THROW IT AT ME IN CLASS?

WHY NOT JUST GIVE IT TO ME NOW?

WHERE WOULD THE FUN BE IN THAT?!

He was right though — my 'arty friend' was definitely interested in entering. Imagine the Art Avenger having their work on permanent display outside the town hall. Rather than just being someone who pranks classmates and gets back at teachers, the Art Avenger would be an actual proper artist like Banksy. All I needed was a good idea.

I'M DEFINITELY GOING TO ENTER THIS COMPETITION. I JUST NEED SOME INSPIRATION.

IN FACT, THAT WOULD BE A GOOD NAME FOR THE NEXT CHAPTER.

CHAPTER 24

INSPIRATION

I thought the best place to look for an idea would be my art books — they hadn't let me down so far. I flicked through, and there were loads of great sculptures in there. I really liked the giant shiny jelly bean made by Anish Kapoor. But nothing felt quite right for a plinth outside Wormwood Town Hall.

FACT FILE: ANISH KAPOOR

He is a British-Indian modern artist who makes loads of cool sculptures.

BLACKEST BLACK

This one is called *Cloud Gate* but it's nickname is 'The Bean'.

He helped make the blackest-ever black paint.

When you paint with it, it looks like a really deep hole.

DON'T FALL IN!

I needed to go down and look at the empty plinth in person to get a feel for it. I got on my bike and headed to the town hall.

My bike is a hand-me-down from Travis, but originally it was the delivery bike for Theo Heath's Butchers.

Travis got it when Theo Heath's was closing down and they were trying to sell everything off cheap. Travis got a bike and the whole family got mince in EVERY meal for a month.

MINCE SANDWICHES, ANYONE?

This all happened around the time Travis was trying to get in with Mitch Conway and the cool kids in his year.

Mitch and his friends all play in a band, but back then they were stuck for a good name. After making a few alterations to the sign on his bike, Travis came up with the name 'The Death Butchers'.

THE DEATH BUTCHERS

Mitch loved the name and invited Travis to join the band. But, as he could only play the maracas, Travis sort of became the band's roadie instead. The bike wasn't ideal for carrying loads of gear, but you could strap three amps on the back if you balanced them just right. Plus, the front basket was perfect for Travis's maracas.

The Death Butchers never officially kicked Travis out of the band but they did go on a tour across Europe without telling him. I think they must be doing OK because one of their songs is in an advert for a supermarket.

SUPASHOP – THE ONLY SUPERMARKET THAT ROCKS!

To this day, Travis still claims that he's a member of the Death Butchers and he's just waiting for them to write a song that needs maracas. But, if you've ever heard their music, you'll know that he's going to be waiting a long time.

WE'LL DEFINITELY HAVE SOME MARACAS ON THE NEXT ALBUM, I PROMISE.

When I got down to the town hall, there was a crane taking down a statue from one of the two plinths. It was Jeremiah Wormwood, one of the two brothers who founded the town.

I'm not sure what he did, but it must be pretty bad if his statue is being pulled down.

The worst thing I've ever done was the time I made my own stink bomb. A few years ago I got an empty jam jar and filled it with stuff I found in the kitchen: tinned sardines, milk, soy sauce and yeast. Then I left it in the garden shed to 'brew' — except I forgot all about it.

I was reminded of it again, though, when there was a huge bang in the garden on a particularly hot day. We all rushed out to the shed to see what it was and when Dad opened the door we were hit by a wall of smell. To this day the garden shed and all Dad's tools have a yeasty fishy aroma. Whatever Jeremiah Wormwood did must have been at least ten times worse than that.

Although Jeremiah was now lying on the ground, his brother, Walter Wormwood, was still standing on the other plinth. Well, not actually him — he died three hundred and something years ago — I obviously mean the statue of him. I looked at the statue of Walter Wormwood, trying to get inspiration, but nothing came to me. Then I looked over to the empty plinth, but still nothing. When I looked back at Walter for a second time, I noticed a pigeon perched on top of his head.

This made a pretty stupid thought pop into MY head. You know how pigeons always like to sit on top of statues? Well, what if I made a

sculpture of a giant pigeon and put a tiny
Walter Wormwood sitting on top of its head?
Pretty stupid, I know, but the more I thought
about it, the more sense it seemed to make. It
was exactly the opposite of when you say a
word over and over until it starts to sound
weird. (If you've never done that before, give it
a go now. Keep repeating the word 'purple' out
loud — I guarantee after about twenty times
you'll start to doubt whether 'purple' is
actually a word at all.)

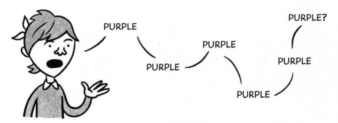

Anyway, where was I? Ah, yes, the pigeon
statue with a small Walter Wormwood on it.
This idea WASN'T as stupid as I'd first thought.
In fact, it might have been borderline genius.

I was excited. I needed to get my idea down on
paper and entered into the competition as soon
as possible.

I raced back home without stopping. Judging by the kind of people who complimented my bike, the Death Butchers are no longer as cool as they used to be.

OH LOOK, GILES – THE DEATH BUTCHERS! WE LIKE THEM, DON'T WE?

YES, DARLING. THAT SONG ON THE SUPERMARKET ADVERT IS PARTICULARLY GROOVY!

CHAPTER 25

DO IT YOURSELF

I got out my special squared paper and looked for my best pencil. I didn't want to jinx it, but I had a feeling that my design could be the one they went with. I also had a feeling that Dylan had been in my room because when I found my favourite pencil it had teeth marks all down it.

GNAW!

I drew out my pigeon-sculpture idea and it looked pretty sweet. Then I made a list of names that I could call my sculpture.

```
NAMES FOR MY
PIGEON SCULPTURE

• SUPER MASSIVE PIGEON
• PECKING ORDER
• IN A FLAP
• COOOOOO, THAT'S
  A BIG PIGEON
• BIG BIRD, SMALL MAN
• FLIPPING THE BIRD
```

I decided on *The Pigeon of Perspective* and I
signed it 'The Art Avenger'.

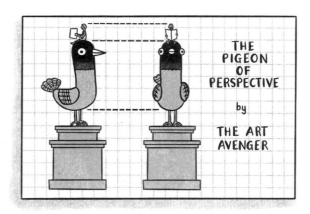

I put my drawing in an envelope, then I got
ready to get back on my bike and post it
through the town-hall letter box. As I was
about to leave my room, though, I saw the

street-art book GeeGee had given me and I had a thought.

Banksy, Invader and any of those other cool street artists that I saw at the exhibition wouldn't enter the competition and wait to have their idea rejected. They'd take matters into their own hands and put up their sculptures without getting permission first. So that's exactly what I was going to do.

This was going to be a seriously big art project, so I decided the best thing to do was to base myself in the loft. There was loads of stuff up there that I could use, plus I would be less likely to get interrupted. Dylan is always barging into my room uninvited so this seemed like a good idea.

Although, having said that, the loft stairs are no deterrent for Dylan — he is an expert climber.

I solved the Dylan problem by putting a jelly baby on each step of the loft ladder. Dylan developed a fear of jelly babies when we camped out in Grandma and Grandad's back garden a few summer holidays ago.

Mum and Dad and the grown-ups were all in the house and to keep us quiet they'd given us each a bag of sweets.

Dylan was sitting in the tent, happily making his way through a bag of jelly babies. He accidentally dropped one but picked it straight back up and put it in his mouth. It wasn't until he started to chew it that he realized it wasn't actually a jelly baby — it was a slug.

Since then, if any of us even say the words 'jelly' and 'babies' together, Dylan starts to lose it.

Up in the loft, I found a load of useful things to make my sculpture with. There was the old plastic baby bath that all three of us had, at some point, been dunked in. Plus the cardboard tube that our Christmas tree came in, an old sleeping bag that was leaking feathers, and tons of other stuff.

The plan was to arrange various objects into the shape of a giant pigeon and then coat it all in paper mache. Then I would cover the whole thing in feathers from the sleeping bag and finally paint it all in pigeon colours.

I made the paper mache in a foot spa that I found. Getting the foot spa back up the loft ladder filled with water was tricky.

Luckily there were already loads of old newspapers up in the loft that Dad had kept. They were all from times when his football team had won a cup or a league or something. I was pretty sure he wouldn't miss them.

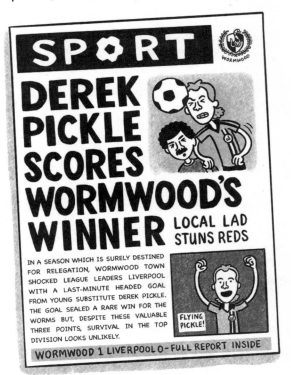

I hope no one ever wants to use the foot spa again because it got pretty gunked up.

I'm not gonna lie — things did get quite messy up there with the glue, water, newspaper, paint and feathers. I figured that I wouldn't have to tidy up in a hurry, though, as no one ever goes up in the loft.

After a few evenings of hard work, my pigeon looked pretty good.

I still needed a little Walter Wormwood to sit on the pigeon's head but luckily for me there was an old suitcase filled with Dad's Action Soldier dolls. When we were younger, he used to have them in a display cabinet in the living room but Mum said it was 'about time he grew up' and she made him put them all up in the loft.

YOU'RE FORTY-FOUR, NOT FOURTEEN.

The one that looked most like Walter Wormwood was called 'Army Officer Action Soldier'. I had to use scissors to get him out of his packaging, and then I gave him a coat of grey paint to make him look like a mini statue.

I put mini Walter on top of my pigeon and stood back to admire my work. It was at that moment that I realized the one major flaw in my plan: my sculpture was too big to get down the loft hatch.

CHAPTER 26

HATCHING A PLAN

This 'small hatch/big bird' scenario reminded me of the time Dad bought a sofa but he didn't check to see if it would fit through our front door. Mum was not pleased. Uncle Steve came over to help and they ended up taking out the front-room window.

THERE'S ONLY ONE THING FOR IT . . .

LOSE THE WINDOW?

Eventually they did get the sofa in but only after a lot of swearing. Then, when they tried to put the window back in, they smashed the glass. It was three days before a replacement could get fitted. Unfortunately, this all happened during one of the coldest Februarys on record.

MUUUUM! TRIXIE'S HOGGING THE HOT-WATER BOTTLE!

I sat down in the loft and tried to work out what to do but quickly got sidetracked looking through our old memory boxes. These are the boxes where Mum keeps all the stuff she doesn't want to chuck out but she also doesn't want cluttering up the house. Travis, Dylan and me have one each and they are filled with stuff like school certificates, photos and cute drawings we made when we were little. I looked through mine and saw the potty chart.

The potty chart is behind probably the most embarrassing story that Mum ever tells about me. Also, it is pretty much the first story she tells anytime she meets a new friend of mine.

When I was learning to get out of nappies,
Mum and Dad made this chart for me. Basically,
every time I successfully used the potty I got
a gold star to stick on the potty chart.
According to Mum, the novelty of gold stars
wore off for me pretty quick, so they started
using chocolate buttons as an incentive instead.
The rule was that each time I did a number one
in the potty I got one chocolate button as a
reward. If I did a number two, however, I would
get two chocolate buttons.

NRRGGG!

THE RULES

A NUMBER ONE =
ONE CHOCOLATE BUTTON

A NUMBER TWO =
TWO CHOCOLATE BUTTONS

I was a smart toddler though, and I quickly
worked out a way to get FOUR chocolate
buttons. Every time I needed a number two, I
would sit down on the potty but, instead of

letting it all come out in one go, I would pinch off the tiniest pebble of poo. Mum would inspect it and reluctantly hand over two chocolate buttons. Then, as soon as I'd eaten them, I'd sit back down and let out the rest so she had to give me two more.

Dad took a weird kind of pride in me doing that. I think he saw it as a sign that when I grew up I'd be good with numbers or something.

HI, IS THAT THE SCHOOL FOR GIFTED CHILDREN? I THINK MY DAUGHTER MIGHT WELL BE A GENIUS.

Sorry if that was too much information, but you can see why I said it was embarrassing. I do have a similar story that, whenever I tell it, embarrasses Mum but I'll save that for later.

Bizarrely, thinking about those chocolate buttons helped me come up with a solution to my current problem. I decided I would cut my sculpture into smaller chunks too. Then, when I got it in place on top of the plinth, I'd reassemble it with super-strong duct tape.

I used Dad's Stanley knife to chop the pigeon into three hatch-friendly pieces.

I always find it funny that Dad gives his tools names, but I guess that's the kind of thing that passes for entertainment when you're a grown-up.

STANLEY, ARE YOU READY FOR SOME CUTTING ADVENTURES?

I also find it strange that he only gives some of his tools names and not all of them. First there is Stanley the knife, which I guess Dad must have named after a great-grandad or something. He calls the keys that he uses to put flat-pack furniture together 'Alan'. This is super odd because there are five of them and they are all different sizes, but he still calls all of them Alan. Surely it would be better to call them something like Barry, Gary, Harry, Larry and Colin, but maybe that's just me.

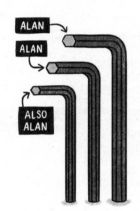

ALAN

ALAN

ALSO ALAN

Finally, and just as weird, is the fact that he's only given one of his screwdrivers a name — the one with a cross-shaped end. He calls that one Phillip, but the one with a flat end doesn't have a name. It would make much more sense if Phillip was the flat one and the cross one was called Chris.

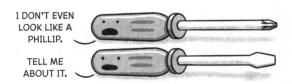

I DON'T EVEN LOOK LIKE A PHILLIP.

TELL ME ABOUT IT.

I suppose when I'm old enough to have my own tools I'll get to call them whatever I like.

Anyway, to cut a long story short, I had cut my long pigeon short. I was now ready to bike down to the town hall.

CHAPTER 27

AVENGER ASSEMBLES

Strapping the pigeon chunks to my bike was tricky. I started to wish I'd paid more attention to Grandad when he kept trying to teach us about tying knots.

RIGHT, KIDS, COME OVER HERE AND I'LL SHOW YOU HOW TO TIE A DOUBLE HALF-HITCH KNOT.

One thing I have learned about old people is that they really like to teach you stuff. They also love giving advice, although not all of it is useful stuff like knot-tying.

Grandma's advice always seems to revolve around vinegar. I'm pretty sure she is a sales rep for the British Vinegar Corporation.

Grandad told me he learned about all the different knots when he was stationed on a battleship during the Second World War. But Dad said Grandad wasn't even alive when the

Second World War was happening and he probably learned them in the Sea Scouts or something. That's the other thing about old people: they like to stretch the truth.

Once everything was tied to my bike, I rode down to the town hall. There were still a couple of people around but I wasn't too worried about anyone seeing me. I figured they'd just think it was a promo stunt for a new Death Butchers song.

When I got to the plinth, it was far too high for me to get on. I tried to use my bike as a ladder but it wasn't tall enough.

I looked around and saw the crane they'd used to take down Jeremiah Wormwood's statue. The guy operating the crane the other day hadn't exactly looked like a genius, so I guessed I could figure it out.

DEFINITELY NOT EINSTEIN

It was a bit like one of those grabber machines you get at the funfair. I pressed the big red button and the crane powered up. Then I spun the arm round till it was pointing at the plinth. All I had to do was extend the arm out a little and I had a perfect route on to the plinth. I remember thinking, 'If this whole art thing goes belly-up, at least there'll be a job for me operating cranes.'

Next, I channelled my inner Dylan and got climbing. The arm part of the crane wasn't too bad, but the chain part had this greasy gunk on it.

After a few journeys, I'd got all the pieces on the plinth and I'd reassembled the pigeon jigsaw with my super-strong duct tape. It was like a final challenge in a crazy game show that Mr Grimes would watch.

... AND NOW, FOR EVERYONE'S FAVOURITE ROUND, IT'S TIME TO ... REASSEMBLE THE PIGEON!!!

I finished off the sculpture by putting the mini Walter Wormwood on top, then I climbed down to get a good look at my sculpture.

WALTER WORMWOOD

THE DEATH BUTCHERS

It was a bit underwhelming — the pigeon had definitely seemed a lot bigger when it was in the loft. I thought it might look a bit better if I stuck some extra feathers over the joins so I decided to go back up the crane arm one more time. But perhaps I should have quit while I was ahead.

I climbed across the arm of the crane no problem, but the greasy gunk on the chain made my hands slippery. About halfway down, I lost my grip completely and started to plummet towards the plinth.

Just when I thought I was going to end up a crumpled heap of broken bones, my jumper got caught on the hook. I ended up swinging from the crane covered in glue and feathers – I looked just like a human piñata.

THIS WAS DEFINITELY NOT IN THE PLAN.

GLUE

I remember thinking two things as I dangled in mid-air. Firstly: wouldn't it have been great if some of that useless advice Grandad was always giving me had covered this exact scenario? And secondly: how on earth am I going to get down from here?

I didn't have to wonder on the second one for too long. I heard a ripping noise as my jumper started to slowly tear. I didn't break any bones, but I did end up breaking the not-quite-big-enough paper-mache pigeon. It was a much better crash mat than it was a sculpture.

My plan to put up my pigeon statue without permission had been a horrific failure. It was back to the drawing board, literally.

CHAPTER 28

WAITING... WAITING... WAITING...

I know it wasn't a very Banksy thing to do, but I decided that perhaps it was best to go down the official channels after all. I got my original pigeon-statue drawing out from my top-secret hiding place and posted it through the town-hall letter box. Then all I could do was cross my fingers and wait.

While we are waiting, do you remember when I said I had a story similar to the potty-chart one, except this one gets Mum embarrassed? I think this is probably an appropriate time to tell it to you.

It was when I was out of nappies but still didn't have that much toilet experience. Mum had taken me to Hadderley's and after about three hours of waiting outside changing rooms watching her try on clothes, I really needed a poo. Mum took me down the escalators to the toilets on the ground floor, then waited outside the cubicle while I went inside and tried to go. Mum heard a lot of straining, a long, squeaky fart and then, finally, a really loud splash. She got all excited, started clapping her hands proudly and said:

PLOPPP! SPLASH!

WELL DONE, TRIXIE! YOU USED THE BIG GIRL'S TOILET! I'M SO PROUD OF YOU!

I shouted back to her:

BUT I
HAVEN'T
BEEN YET!

About two minutes later, a woman came out of
the cubicle next to me — I don't know who had
the redder face, her or Mum.

My long and boring wait to hear about the
sculpture competition soon became even more
long and boring. I'd completely forgotten about
the mess I'd left up in the loft. When Dad saw

it, he flipped. I've got a feeling Dylan might have tipped him off.

DAAAAAAAD, TRIXIE DID A MESS-MESS UP THERE!

My punishment was originally to tidy the place up, which I could just about handle, but when Dad discovered Army Officer Action Soldier had been taken out of his pack and painted grey, I wasn't allowed to go out for two weeks. Apparently that thing was worth some serious money.

One thing this punishment did give me was a chance to think about my time as the Art Avenger. The heat had died down at school and Mr Chippenham had been forced to give up on

his investigation after Mrs McGovern heard
about some of his unusual methods.

HOW MANY TIMES,
CLIFFORD? YOUR
CUPBOARD IS FOR
STATIONERY AND
STATIONERY ALONE.

Overall, even though things like *The Stink-pipe
Bully*, *Basketball Spewmageddon* and *The Horse
Poo in Chippenham's Parking Spot* had been huge
successes, to the kids at school they were
merely stupid pranks.

THAT ART AVENGER
IS REALLY FUNNY.

YEAH – THE
BASKETBALL-BARF
THING WAS HILARIOUS!

In my eyes, though, they were works of art.
If only I could share my secret identity with
someone who would completely get it. Rory
knowing about me was OK, I supposed, but he
would never truly appreciate my missions on an
artistic level. I started to think that maybe, as
it was Auntie GeeGee who'd first set me off on
my Art Avenger journey, I should give her a call
and tell her all about it. I was pretty sure
she'd understand much more than Rory or Beeks
or anyone else at school.

I'VE GOT SOMETHING
TO TELL YOU . . .

Before I had a chance to feel any more sorry
for myself, the *Wormwood Post* came through
our letter box. On the front page was a big
story about a 'plinth-reveal party' on Saturday.

Had they chosen my pigeon design? It was definitely a long shot but you never know – stranger things have happened. The thought of actually having my art unveiled in front of everyone started to give me

butterflies in my stomach.

CHAPTER 29

THE BIG REVEAL

The big day finally came. I decided to knock for
Beeks to see if he fancied going down to the
town hall with me. Weirdly, he seemed super
eager, but that all made sense when he told
me that he'd also entered the plinth
competition. Firstly, I couldn't believe he'd
entered without telling me. Secondly,
I wouldn't have been surprised

TYPICAL!

if they'd only gone and picked
whatever design Beeks had come
up with. The way my luck
had been going lately,
I could've fallen into a
bucket of lollipops and come
out sucking my thumb.

It also got me thinking: if Beeks had entered, then just how many other people had too?

When we got down to the town hall, people were putting up bunting, and there was a stage where Mayor Tafazolli would announce the winner.

Dad always calls Mayor Tafazolli 'Mayor Toffee Apple'. At first I thought it was just because 'Tafazolli' and 'toffee apple' sound sort of similar but I later found out it's because Dad says he has 'a stick up his bum'. That is only a saying, though. He doesn't actually have a stick up his bum (as far as I know).

Apparently the mayor rejected Dad's planning application for a garage. Let's just say Dad's not the mayor's biggest fan, and whenever he sees the mayor in the newspaper he says stuff like: '******** *** ***** ******* ******* **** **
******* ***** ******* !'

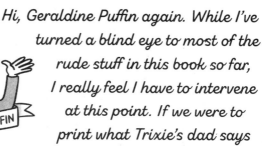

Hi, Geraldine Puffin again. While I've turned a blind eye to most of the rude stuff in this book so far, I really feel I have to intervene at this point. If we were to print what Trixie's dad says about Mayor Tafazolli, we would be inundated with complaints from parents, teachers and librarians and we do not want that. I hope you understand.

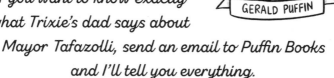

Hi, Gerald Puffin again. I just want to apologize for my wife, Geraldine. She can be a bit of an old fuddy-duddy sometimes. If you want to know exactly what Trixie's dad says about Mayor Tafazolli, send an email to Puffin Books and I'll tell you everything.

Anyway, let's get back to the plinth-reveal party.

There was a big wooden box over the top of
the plinth. Me and Beeks tried to get a closer
look, but we got told to buzz off by the
crane operator.

BEAT IT,
YOU TWO!

We went for a quick walk around instead and
it was already getting busy. The Burgers and
More van was setting up, the Taco Wagon was
serving customers, and Pedro's Pizzas also had
a stall. It seemed like everyone was trying to
cash in on the big reveal.

A Wormwood FM van with some really tinny speakers was parked up. They had a jingle that promised 'non-stop hits' but it was more like one song followed by about twelve adverts.

We walked back towards the stage and it seemed as though, in the ten minutes that we'd been looking around, the entire population of Wormwood had turned up. Everyone was there and I mean EVERYONE.

Spencer Smedley was there.

Mr Grimes was there.

CAN'T THEY HURRY THIS ALONG? I'VE GOT TO BE BACK FOR *CASH LADDERS* AT EIGHT O'CLOCK.

Mr Chippenham was there.

I DROVE DOWN HERE IN MY VINTAGE CAR. HAVE I TOLD YOU ABOUT MY VINTAGE CAR?

Dudley Davis was there.

WHAT'S A PLINTH?

Rory McGory was there.

CUDDLY DAVIS!

Grandma was there.

Grandad was there.

ANYONE FANCY SOME WARM VINEGAR?

WHEN YOU'RE GOING ON HOLIDAY, PUT A SHOE IN EACH SUITCASE SO IF ONE SUITCASE GETS STOLEN, THE THIEF CAN'T WEAR THEM.

Suranna Adebayo
was there.

I CALCULATE THERE ARE APPROXIMATELY THREE HUNDRED AND EIGHTY-SEVEN PEOPLE HERE.

Mr Woodhouse
was there.

WE'RE BACK FROM OUR ALPACA TREK. WHAT DID WE MISS?

Mum and Dad
were there.

SOUTH AFRICAN SAUSAGE, DARLING?

Mrs Dewson
was there.

AS IT'S SATURDAY, I'M SKIPPING MY SOUP-IN-A-CUP AND TREATING MYSELF TO A PEDRO'S PIZZA.

Travis and Dylan
were there.

THIS IS BORING.

Mr James
was there.

AND III-EEEE III...
...WILL ALWAYS LOVE YOOOOO OOU

Derren Devlin was there.

The Death Butchers were there. They were all set up on the stage and they had their amps cranked up to eleven.

They started playing one of their early songs and Dad, Uncle Steve and Mr O'Neal all started talking about how music was 'much better in our day'. Well, I've been on car journeys with Dad and the only way his music is better is if you are looking for a way to bore people into a coma.

♫ ...HEAVEN KNOWS ♫ I'M MISERABLE NOW ♫ ♫

THIS ONE'S A CLASSIC, KIDS.

Things changed when the band started playing their supermarket-advert song. All the old people in the crowd clapped along in time — the Death Butchers had officially sold out.

I think the penny finally dropped for Travis that he was definitely NOT a member of the band when Mitch Conway said they were going to play 'a song written especially for our newer fans' and then pulled out a pair of maracas.

After the band finished playing, Mayor Tafazolli got up on the stage. He said it was time to announce the winner, but then he went off on

a rambling speech all about the history of
Wormwood.

I realized that a lot of people must've entered
the competition, so my chances of actually
winning would be pretty small. But for some
strange reason, don't ask me why, I just knew
that I had won. Without wanting to sound all
Star Wars about it, I felt like it was my destiny.
I had gone from thinking art was sucky to
becoming our school's most talked-about artist.
It seemed like winning this competition was
surely the next step on my art journey.

I started getting a strange tingling feeling and
had a weird daydream premonition of the
mayor opening an envelope and reading out my
name. I guessed this must be what it was like

to have spidey-sense. I quickly snapped out of it, though, when the mayor got to the business end of his speech.

AND NOW THE MOMENT WE'VE ALL BEEN WAITING FOR . . .

THE WINNING SCULPTURE WAS CHOSEN BECAUSE WE THINK IT WILL MAKE YOU ALL SMILE WHENEVER YOU WALK PAST IT.

IT ALSO BRINGS A LITTLE BIT OF NATURE TO OUR TOWN CENTRE.

WE WERE REALLY IMPRESSED WITH THE DESIGN BUT WE DON'T ACTUALLY KNOW A LOT ABOUT THE ARTIST.

IT APPEARS THEY ARE QUITE SECRETIVE AND THEY GO BY A MADE-UP NAME . . .

ANYWAY, THAT'S ENOUGH BUILD-UP – CRANES, PLEASE!

Then the mayor signalled to the guy operating the crane, who started to slowly lift the box that was covering the plinth. This was it — this was finally it. This was the moment that the Art Avenger would become a recognized, official, 100-per-cent-legit artist.

Just as the box was almost above the plinth, the mayor announced:

AND THE WINNING SCULPTURE IS . . .

HAPPINESS WORM BY THE BLUE HAND!

What the? *Happiness Worm?* The Blue Hand? Who on earth was the Blue Hand?

I looked at the plinth, and there stood a ten-foot-tall worm, just like the one on the Wormwood town crest, except this one was bright blue, smiling and wearing shades.

I've got to admit that, although I was gutted about not winning, this WAS a great sculpture. The mayor was right: it did make me smile when I looked at it, and using the worm from the town crest was a genius idea. Why didn't I think of that?

Then I started to get a horrible feeling. What if the Blue Hand was Beeks? This wasn't how it was supposed to be. I was the one who'd spent the last few months using the power of art to right wrongs and bring villains to justice, and now Beeks had jumped in at the last minute to grab the glory . . .

THE NAME'S BEEKS BUT YOU CAN JUST CALL ME 'THE GREATEST ARTIST WORMWOOD HAS EVER SEEN'.

I turned to confront him but, as I opened my mouth, a familiar face caught my eye through the crowd. It was Miss Handley. She smiled at me and waved. As she did, I noticed her hand was covered in blue paint.

The Blue Hand. Of course! It made complete sense. Miss Handley walked towards me through the crowd.

SO DO YOU LIKE THE SCULPTURE THEN, TRIXIE? OR, SHOULD I SAY, DO YOU LIKE THE SCULPTURE THEN, ART AVENGER?

WAIT, YOU KNOW?

OF COURSE I KNOW! I'VE KNOWN ALL ALONG. EVER SINCE YOUR *STINK-PIPE BULLY* PAINTING. I'VE GOT TO SAY, THE INSTALLATION IN MR CHIPPENHAM'S PARKING SPACE WAS INSPIRED!

THANKS, AND I LOVE YOUR SCULPTURE TOO. BUT I DON'T UNDERSTAND: WHY DO YOU CALL YOURSELF THE BLUE HAND? WHY NOT JUST MISS HANDLEY?

WELL, SCHOOLS CAN BE A BIT FUNNY ABOUT HIRING A SUBSTITUTE TEACHER WHO IS ALSO A STREET ARTIST, SO I TRY TO KEEP THEM BOTH SEPARATE.

OH ...

BUT THAT DOESN'T MATTER NOW. MR WOODHOUSE IS BACK SO I GUESS I'LL BE MOVING ON.

WAIT, SO I'VE ONLY JUST DISCOVERED WHO YOU REALLY ARE AND NOW YOU'RE GOING?

She handed me a card and then, just like in the movies, she disappeared off into the crowd.

It was more like a superhero movie than an actual superhero movie. I even started to check for cameras, to make sure I wasn't secretly being filmed without realizing it.

There were no cameras and there was no Miss Handley.

CHAPTER 30

THE END BIT

So, there you go: although I didn't win the competition, I did find out that I wasn't alone. There is another Art Avenger I can call upon if I ever need help — well, not quite an Art Avenger, a Blue Hand, but you know what I mean. Imagine the different art missions we could get up to if we teamed up.

QUICK, THERE'S A BANK ROBBERY IN PROGRESS!

WE'RE GONNA NEED DOUBLE-SIDED STICKY TAPE!

Although, having said that, would the Blue Hand actually want to team up with the Art Avenger? Maybe she's one of those superheroes who always goes it alone?

Who knows? These are the kinds of questions that may or may not get answered in the next Art Avenger book, which, if you've enjoyed this one, you should definitely buy.

GERALDINE PUFFIN

I just want to say that I wholeheartedly agree with this. You should definitely buy the next Art Avenger book.

And I just want to say that this is one of those very rare occasions when I completely agree with my wife.

GERALD PUFFIN

What I can say for certain is that being the
Art Avenger is a lot of fun and I'm definitely
not stopping here. Also, Beeks and me have
already started work on *Blammo* number two
and we've got some great new comic strips
that we can't wait to show you.

I started this book by saying that art is sucky
and you know what? It is pretty sucky. But only
if you are a bully, or a teacher who rips up
comics, or a PE teacher who doesn't let girls
play basketball, or a vain, mean show-off with
a talking watch.

On the flip side, art is 100 per cent not sucky if you are a child who doesn't want to get run over by a car, or a depressed dog, or a kid who doesn't want to be bullied (or a bully who deep down doesn't actually want to be a bully).

That's it — that's the end of the book.

I'm off now.

Bye.

See ya.

Au revoir. (That's 'bye' in French.)

Why are you still here?

Honestly, that's it.

Stop reading.

It's 100 per cent finished.

This isn't like the movies where there's an extra bit after the credits.

This is definitely it.

This is the end.

Why are you still reading?

Don't you believe me?

Please, put down the book and stop reading.

Honestly, when you turn this page there will be no more words.

These are definitely the last words in the book.

Bye.

ABOUT THE AUTHOR:
Olaf Falafel

He is an author, illustrator and stand-up comedian.

Some of his jokes have won awards.

Some of his jokes are rubbish!

HI!

When he was at school, he made a comic called *Bullseye*.

He has two daughters who are a similar age to Trixie.

He sold copies of it in the playground.

He studied art and likes to paint in his spare time.

Olaf loves football!

His favourite team is Luton Town Football Club.

He painted this portrait of Snake, his pet cat.

AS A REWARD FOR GETTING TO THE END
OF THE BOOK, HERE ARE SOME BONUS
BLAMMO COMIC STRIPS FOR YOU!

BUM-FACED SNAILS

I'VE BEEN WAITING AGES. WHERE HAVE YOU BEEN?

NOWHERE.

YOU'VE NOT BEEN IN THE FRUIT BOWL AGAIN, HAVE YOU?

NO.

EARLIER...

NOT VERY CLEVER ALIENS

OH NO! THE TREES ARE ATTACKING!

MY RAIN STICK!

WHY IS THE AIR SO ANGRY?

I MADE A NEW FRIEND!

SHOP

BARRY PLOPPER BOY WIZARD

WE CAN'T FIND THE CHOOSING HAT ANYWHERE!

NOT TO WORRY... CHOOSING HAT REPLACIUM!

WILL THAT DO?

GET IN THE BIN!
by Beeks

OH NO! MY CHOCOLATE BAR!

NOT TO WORRY – FIVE-SECOND RULE.

KITTY LITTER

GET IN THE BIN!!!